DARK &
STORMY

J. Mercer

Published 2017 / Bare Ink
Printed in the United States of America
Library of Congress Control Number: 8435322
Dark & Stormy / written by J Mercer

Cover design © Chris Slabber
Edited by Gina Ardito

For all our wild horses

"The beginnings and endings
of all human undertakings are untidy."

– John Galsworthy

KAI'S ARREST

Kai sank his hands deep in the snow until his flesh burned, hoping the cold would freeze out the fire seething inside. He sank them further, until they were hidden beneath the white, until it seemed he lost them altogether. This was no surprise, as he'd lost everything when he lost her.

The voice beside him, reading him his rights, came in and out on the icy breeze, but Kai didn't hear the words. What he heard was the echo behind them of what his life should have been.

He should've had Faryn.

He should've had a house and a family. He'd been so close, so close to finally considering himself a good human being, and respected. But a house, a family, respect, none of these things would happen for him now, innocent or not. The truth didn't matter at this point, whether he'd done it. What mattered was the policeman pulling him away from her, away from her grave.

What mattered was the blood on his hands.

SPRING

1

A POSITIVE MOVE

Faryn

Sometimes I felt wild and restless, like a mustang that turns around one day and realizes it's been domesticated when all it thought it did was take the offer of a simple apple. It always started the same way, from a point deep in my center, and would grow to an incessant itch I couldn't shake.

To soothe it, I'd been driving for days, all my belongings stacked high behind me in my small SUV. The ones I'd seen as necessities anyway, since my goal was to pare back and succumb to basic need.

I yearned for amnesia to settle on my mind and recreate me into who I was supposed to be, because at thirty-three I didn't know anymore. I'd been so many things, so very split and so widely scattered.

If I chased solitude and eliminated distractions, I figured my true self would have no choice but to rise from the ashes of all the other roles I'd spent my life playing. And if it did, maybe I could go back home and survive the future, whether that entailed the path I'd been on or a new one altogether.

Or maybe I'd find a home here, in this small Midwestern town that spoke to me of fresh beginnings. After an hour of winding along its streets, exploring every corner, I stopped in the driveway of an old brick house that was split into four units. A large cube with many windows, it pulled at me more than the apartment building a few blocks over, or the gaping farmhouse on the edge of town, all three of which had *for rent* signs crookedly staked in their front lawns.

It was manageable and adorable, at least from the outside. All brick, but lighter than the standard red, with faded white windowpanes and a small covering over an even smaller front porch. An attached covered staircase ran up the left side, and an old grill stood sentry on the right.

Perfect.

Fishing my phone out of my bag, I dialed the number written in fat permanent marker beneath the words encouraging me to call. And as if fate had shifted the winds to drop me here, my new landlord was not only home, but able to forgo everything to meet me and hand over the key in ten minutes flat.

While I waited, I wandered the property. There were no bulbs peeking out to meet the spring weather and no carefully tended bushes. I'd always preferred the overgrown, less uniform look anyway, of yews stretching their arms. It seemed unfair to keep them boxed in with garden shears, and, in my opinion, curtailed their ragged allure.

The lawn, though sparse and bumpy, was mowed, and a few ornamental trees lined one side of the yard, hiding the small gas station next door. A tangled, spotted hedge ran along the other side of the lot, and across the street, business after business lined the sidewalk. Not much of a residential area, but I liked being inside a community, instead of on the outskirts.

My new landlord drove a rusted pickup. He chugged into the lot so slowly, I nearly checked for his feet beneath it.

Parking in the center of the graveled space, he hopped out in oil-splattered overalls, his clunky boots hitting the gravel drive with a thump. Walking as slowly as he drove, he made his way to where I leaned against my car, reaching his hand out for mine when he was still a good five feet away.

It made for an awkward moment, him coming at me like that, and I shook his hand as quickly as I could when it finally arrived.

"Thanks for meeting me so quick," I said.

We'd already exchanged pleasantries on the phone. His name was Philip, but he pronounced it *Philp*, and now that we were face to face, I surveyed his long, curly black mullet, thick boxy glasses, and vicious underbite.

"Oh, no problem," he replied. "I'm not doin' much of anything, most o' the time. You need somethin', just call me up, and I'll run right over. That's my job. This here house is my job." He stepped toward the first open unit. Three of the four were available. Opening the door for me, he said, "It's certainly great to meet you, Faryn. Great to see you."

"Yes, um, you too." I squinted at his awkwardness before making my way into the living room. Bare rooms gave me the shivers, and though the space was warm and stuffy from being closed up, I rubbed my hands along my arms to ward off goose bumps.

Philip shuffled past me to take the lead and showed me around not only that apartment, but the two other possibilities as well. The second unit, upstairs on the right, had a strange sort of stink to it, while the third had been left fully furnished by the previous tenant. This last one, second floor left, also had the best light.

Back at my car, I rummaged in my purse for the down payment, handed the hundreds over, and took the key.

"It was great to see you," he blabbered. "Really great to see you. You'll be happy with this place, I'm sure. And it was really nice to meet you. Really nice." He emphasized his sincerity with a toothy grin.

"Thanks, Philip. It was nice meeting you, too. Do you have a card, so I know where to send the rent?"

"Oh, you won't need that." He ran a hand through his bangs. "We don't mail rent around here. I'll be around, you know, working on things. You'll see me plenty. No worries about that."

"Oh. Um, okay."

They did things differently here than where I'd come from, but that's what I'd wanted, right? Small, quaint, and simple. If that meant this creepy landlord of mine would be hanging around and waiting for my rent, well, I was willing to go with it.

Glancing at my car and the boxes pushing against the windows like a small child blowing his cheeks, I said, "Well, I should really get unpacking."

"Hey!" Philip's brows jumped his forehead. "I could help you with that, you know? I might look a little mangy and all, but I got me some muscle under this fat."

I studied him. He actually wasn't all that fat, just slightly chubby. "You know, that's okay. Maybe another time?"

"But you won't be movin' in again later, will ya? There really ain't no other time."

"Yeah, but I've been driving all day. It'll feel good to do some physical work."

He nodded. "You sure do look like you enjoy some physical work."

I raised an eyebrow, but said nothing. Another awkward moment swooped in, and the seconds ticked by as we stared at each other.

"Okay." He nodded. "Well, call if you get tired, you hear?"

"I sure will, Philip. Thanks for everything." And by everything, I meant the apartment.

"Oh, yes, yes. No problem at all. It really was nice to see you. So great to see you." As if he hadn't said that fifty times, and each like a starved puppy lapping up attention.

Against my better judgment, I forced out a tight smile. After a few more beats, he turned on his heel with a little wave, hoisted himself into the cab of his truck, and peeled out faster than he'd meandered in.

When the dust resettled on the driveway, I opened my trunk and got to work.

I'd struck lucky to find a furnished apartment, and a cute one at that. I loved sticky old windows that wouldn't quite shut all the way, a kitchen floor that slanted softly in one direction, ancient wooden floorboards with scuffs and stains, and bathrooms so small you could hardly lift up both arms.

At least, that's what I loved today. Yesterday, I'd loved large great rooms and windows so huge you felt like you were sitting outside. I'd wanted a kitchen massive enough to seat six people around an island, and a laundry room so big it might, just maybe, stay neat with ten pairs of shoes littering the floor—twenty on a bad day.

But today was different. Today it was only me, and I was simple. Or I was trying to be.

Halfway through the box hauling, my neighbor came home. He drove up in an old limo and parked on the other side of the house, right on the grass where he'd already smoothed out two paths for his tires.

Removing himself from the vehicle, he tipped his baseball cap in my direction. As he walked over, I put down the box I was holding and got ready to shake his hand.

"It's been a long time since I've had company around here," he said, his face absent a smile. Long and droopy, he reminded me of a bloodhound.

"I'm Faryn. It's nice to meet you."

"Leon. Nice to meet you, too." He ran his fingers up and down his suspenders and ducked his head to look in my car. "Anything heavy you want some help with?"

"Nah, that's okay." Would everyone around here be so accommodating?

"You sure? I wouldn't mind—Faryn, is it?"

I nodded. Though, there was no creepiness seeping from this one, only melancholy, and he was going to be my neighbor. "I mean, I don't need any help, but if you want. . ."

He shrugged slowly, as if fighting an underwater current. "I ain't got much else to do." Testing out the few boxes ready to be pulled, he grabbed the heaviest. "Faryn sure is a pretty name," he said.

"Thank you, Leon."

"You're welcome." A twitch worked his lips, and I took that as a smile.

We traipsed up the stairs and into my apartment. I pointed toward the living room, which was at the front of the building looking out on the street, and he set the box in there.

"Where you from, Faryn?" he asked on our way back down.

"Where are you from, Leon?"

"From here, of course. Everybody who's here is from here."

"Yeah?"

"Yeah. Who would want to live here enough to move here?"

I couldn't hold it in, his seriousness so complete, that I let out a laugh. "*I* want to live here, I guess."

"Yeah, well, you got another think comin'."

"Philip told me I'd love it here," I said, as he passed me another box.

7

"You mean *Philp?*" Again, he delivered this without a crack of humor.

I grinned. "That is precisely who I mean."

"Yeah, Philp's a chipper fellow. Too chipper for me."

I tilted my head as we took to the stairs, my heart reaching out to him already. "I'll try to remember that. Keep myself somber while you're around."

He looked back with another lip twitch. "Naw, I won't hold your happiness against you."

"Just Philp's?" I asked, fighting another grin.

"Well, he rubs it in everybody's face."

Leon was turning out to be an interesting sort of comedian, I decided, while depositing my box on the kitchen table. He disappeared into the bedroom, and we silently took the steps for another round.

A few more trips and phase one of unpacking was officially complete. I walked him back downstairs and followed him over to his front door. He was on the opposite side of the building from me, on the first floor.

"It's certainly nice to have another body around here," he said. "If you ever see me out grillin', you're always welcome to join me. Eatin' alone can get pretty old."

I eyeballed his grill. It looked like it would fall apart under the weight of a burger. "Thanks, I'll keep that in mind."

Tipping his hat one more time, he made his way inside.

2

STEADY WORK

Faryn

I watched the bar across the street for a few weeks, often with a cup of coffee in hand. The morning after I moved in, they plastered a help wanted sign in the front window, and I'd chewed my lip over it ever since.

I knew nothing of bartending and worried it would be a busy place, but there'd been no rowdy nights and no drunken brawls. In fact, the influx was arguably heaviest during lunch, and the patrons, for the most part, seemed tidy. It was reasonably lazy there, like about everything else in town. The gas station, grocer, and drugstore all ticked to a slower clock than I was accustomed.

After giving them time to recover from their latest midday

rush, I grabbed my keys off the table and locked up, something Leon assured me was unnecessary around here, but a habit I hadn't yet been able to break. Then I made my way across the street.

The spring air smelled sweeter up here, and the flowers blooming from the ornamental trees drew an upswing to my step. I crossed the street, pushed open the door, and was accosted by stale cigarette smoke.

Whoosh. Just like that: sweet and comforting to pungent and appalling.

But it was clean; this was obvious even in the dim light. The windows were long and thin, set high on the wall near the ceiling; the bar short and to the right. An old cigarette machine sat in the far corner, an array of lottery and arcade games banked the wall on my left, and a pool table sat in a wide empty space. About seven tables scattered the rest of the room, and one man sat at the bar while another stood behind it.

They stared at me.

I stood a little straighter and took the seven steps to greet them. "Hi, I'm Faryn Miller." I reached my hand out, but the bartender didn't move so I dropped it. "I saw you were hiring, and I'd like to apply for the job."

"You got it," he said.

"I'm sorry?"

"It's yours." He didn't blink. "Done."

"Don't you want to interview me?"

"You just had your interview."

I looked at the old man on the stool. He shrugged.

"Lewis?" the bartender asked. "You agree, don't cha?"

Lewis nodded and wiped a little drool off the corner of his lip with the rounded end of an amputated forearm. No left hand. "Can she make a Dark and Stormy?"

"Yeah, see, I can't make anything," I admitted. "But I'd really love the job."

"I already gave it to you, sugar." The bartender reached his hand out, and I shook it. "I'm Charles, but you can call me Chuck. All the pretty ladies do. And I own the place, so if I want to hire an inexperienced Greek goddess, well, then that's what I'll do."

I'd never been referred to as a Greek goddess before, so I'd take it, no matter it was coming from a man as slick as this one.

His black hair was smoothed back and gelled down. A silver post hung from one ear and an angel tattoo decorated the front side of his neck, her bottom half hidden under the collar of his black tee. Then again, maybe she wasn't an angel, all voluptuous and scantily clad that she was, but she did have wings. His nose was a shiny beacon of oil, and his hand even felt somewhat slimy in mine, enough that it was taking all I had not to wipe my palm against my jeans.

"A Dark and Stormy?" I asked. "What's that?"

Chuck motioned me behind the bar, and as I rounded the corner I met his snug boot-cut jeans and flashy cowboy boots. He pulled a glass out from under the counter. "A highball glass," he informed, while reaching behind him for a bottle of dark rum and into the glass-fronted fridge for a can of beer. "And ginger beer, purchased solely for this young man in

11

front of us."

He scooped the glass through the ice bin, poured a heavy splash of rum into it, and topped it off with beer. After swiping a precut slice of lime onto the rim from a bowl under the counter, he slid it across to Lewis, who took a sip and licked his lips.

"Now you try," Chuck said.

I did exactly as he had, and we waited for Lewis' approval.

Lewis lifted the glass to his mouth with his good hand—well, his one hand—and took a slow, steady drink. As he set it back down on the bar, he nodded. "Hers is better."

"As well it should be, coming from a pretty lady," Chuck agreed. He brushed past me, a little too close, and removed the sign from the window.

The rest of the afternoon, I was tutored in the art of mixing drinks. Even though, they told me, most of Chuck's customers ordered beer.

I went home at five with instructions to come back in a few hours for the Saturday night crowd. Crossing the lawn, I ran into Leon. He'd been my sole social interaction, aside from a few awkward chats with Philip, and it seemed natural to share the news with him.

"You watch out for Chuck, you hear? He can be a bit handsy."

"No 'Congrats, go you'?" I teased, raising my fists up to emphasize the *go you*.

"Congrats, Faryn, of course." He copied my cheering motion and muttered the rest of it. "Go you."

I folded into laughter. How could a classic melancholic like himself be so funny? Maybe it was all relative; maybe my sister, a bubbling fountain of curiosity, wouldn't find him as amusing as I did.

"But really." He shook a finger at me as I quieted. "I ain't kiddin' about his hands."

Patting his arm, I assured him, "I've dealt with plenty worse than handsy, Leon, but thanks for the warning."

He nodded that underwater nod of his. "Maybe I'll wander over later. Too many people on a Saturday, though. We'll see."

"It'd be great to see a friendly face in the crowd, but if not, we can always celebrate tomorrow over burgers." I'd wandered down last Sunday when he'd been grilling, the scent of the coals and cooking meat too tempting to resist.

"We'll see," he repeated, yanking open his car door which stuck a little. Throwing up a hand, he got in. "Headed to the grocer. You need anything?"

I shook my head. "Thanks, though."

He nodded, then slammed the door, and I stood aside to watch him maneuver out.

I'd been living off snacks mostly, only because cooking for one felt odd and pointless, after all the people I'd fed in my life. It had taken me two torturous, lonely weeks to finally grow accustomed to eating in silence, untethered from conversation be it polite or intimate. But I'd wanted simple, and simple meant cooking for one.

3

GETTING INTO THE SWING OF THINGS
Faryn

I was very familiar with the cheap beers by ten o'clock and felt pretty good about the pace of things—just busy enough to keep my mind at a low hum.

Lewis sat at his stool, and I got the impression he was careful not to abandon it. So far, I'd learned he was retired, had lost his hand in a farming accident way back, and drove a new boat of a car, versus an old one. Those were his words. The car was a source of pride for him, and Chuck wasted no time bragging about his in turn.

"I'll take you out back to see it," Chuck said, waggling his eyebrows, "whenever you want." It was, supposedly, a shiny apple red Camaro.

I would take him up on that eyebrow waggle about never, not that I was even sure he could peel himself out of those tight jeans to actually make it happen. But overall, as a boss, he wasn't so bad.

Chuck got preoccupied with a couple at the other end of the bar, so I leaned over to Lewis and his sparse, wispy hair. "I'd take your new boat of a car over a loud Camaro any day."

He perked up at this, his watery blue eyes twinkling in the dim light. "It's a solid car, hasn't done me wrong yet. And it'll last longer than I will, that's for sure."

A group of women caught my eye from one of the tables, so I gathered them more drinks. When I came back, Lewis was staring into his half-filled glass.

I settled back into what I was coming to think of as my place at the bar, and he looked up to commend me on my work. "You sure do make a good Dark and Stormy, Faryn."

"At least I'm doing something right," I responded with a wink. This embarrassed him, and he hid his gaze back in his glass.

As I pondered his life, and who might be waiting for him at home, I drummed my fingertips against my thigh. The music was louder now than it had been earlier, and the din a harsher rumble with more patrons filling the space, but still I noticed every time the door opened and shut.

It created a vacuum, a momentary pause in which everyone stopped to glance over and see who it was. Because they all knew each other, of course. With every new entry came at least one wave, a handful of head nods, and an occasional shout of welcome that did its best to carry itself across the room, pushing through both the conversations and the beating notes tumbling relentlessly out of the speakers.

No one sat at the bar aside from Lewis, they only approached to order, and I wondered if it was me, the new girl, who kept them congregated on the other side of the room. Chuck and Lewis didn't act like it was anything out of the ordinary though, so I pushed aside the paranoia to chat with Lewis and watch the crowd.

Until the moment the door would open and we would all turn in its direction. Then back to what we were doing. Then who was leaving. Then back to what we were doing. Then pouring beers, pulling cans from the fridge, uncapping bottles, whatever their poison. And back to the door, whenever it chose to grab our attention.

This meant that I, along with everyone else, saw him the moment he walked in.

A good few inches taller than me, and muscular, he might as well have had misfit written all over him. His jeans fit him perfectly, unlike most of the other men in here who'd gone too tight, too baggy, or too short. Exposed beneath his black leather jacket was a green tee, and a heavy cross hung on a thick chain from his neck. Dark uncomplicated hair and strong, shaded facial features bespoke of an exotic lineage on at least one side. That stood out here, against the solid cream-colored background, which was perhaps why everyone else's eyes lingered on him a moment longer than normal, too.

He was beautiful. Not that it should matter. The last thing I needed was a lover.

A much less attractive girl hung off him, tall and skinny

with severely cut, shoulder length blonde hair—very blonde, unnaturally blonde—and a pointy beak of a nose. Her ensemble began with a lacy white shirt over a black bra, skinny black jeans, and bowling shoes, only to end with large hoop earrings, a pretty shade of pink on her lips, and a black studded belt.

They made their way over to me, them and another man who was nearly consumed by the pockmarks on his face.

The misfit flashed a wicked half smile, only furthering his effect on me. "You're new here," he said.

"I am," I responded. "Can I get you a drink?"

"I mean, you're new in town," he replied.

"I'm that, too."

He reached his hand out, a first for the night. Everyone had verbally pegged me for the displaced person I was, and though most had taken the initiative to introduce themselves, none had offered a proper handshake. Well, none since Chuck, but this hand, from this stranger, was a world away from the limp, moist hand of my boss.

"I'm Kai," he said. "It's a pleasure."

"I'm Faryn, and the pleasure is mine." I truly was not trying to weasel my way between him and his girlfriend. This had always been my standard response when faced with that line. The blonde wasn't going to like me anyway, I could already tell by the angled expression narrowing her face.

"I'm Savannah," she smacked out in a harsh tone. "Savvy for short. And this is Andy."

Andy winked at me, and I winked dramatically back. He smiled a lazy pimp smile in response, Savannah rolled her eyes, and Kai chuckled into his shoulder, perhaps the only one catching the fact that I was making fun of his friend's lame hello.

But that wasn't very nice of me. Sometimes I didn't recognize myself. "Can I get you a drink, Andy?" I asked, to make it up to him.

"I'll take whatever you're serving," he replied, somewhat lewdly.

"How about a Dark and Stormy?"

Lewis looked up with a grin. I smiled back at him, resisting the urge to wink once again.

"What's that?" Andy asked.

"It comes highly recommended by Lewis here."

Lewis lifted his glass and nodded, before throwing back the rest of the amber liquid.

"That's what you're always drinking?" Savannah asked him.

"I'll try one," Kai said, and my stomach curled.

Seriously, I did not need a lover.

I looked pointedly at Savannah, a dare, and she curled her lip at me.

"Why not?" She nudged Andy with her piercingly sharp elbow, and I winced.

He shrugged. "Sure, why not?"

"Lewis?" I asked.

"Bring it on, girlie." He slid the glass over to me and I caught it, something else I'd become proficient at that evening. After setting three more next to it, I mixed more of this drink I now knew so well.

Chuck had scolded me for reusing Lewis' glass but I'd

explained how it saved water and dishwashing soap, and thus the environment. Lewis thought it a fantastic idea, and I assured Chuck I wouldn't touch the pour spout to the contaminated surface, so he threw up his hands and let me continue.

I honestly wasn't sure how this old man could consume such a vast amount of alcohol and still seem so utterly sober. Or maybe he hadn't been sober in twenty years.

Kai watched me closely, as did Savannah, and Andy's eyes roamed the room. Ice, rum, beer, lime, I could now do this in my sleep. Presenting them with a flourish and a curtsy, I pushed Lewis' back to him and let the others grab the one they wanted.

Kai went for the drink closest to me, and I watched his fingers as they slowly brought the drink toward him, his hand as he lifted it to his lips, his lips until they disappeared under the liquid, his eyes until they connected with mine.

Guilty, my gaze fluttered to Savannah. She was watching us over the rim of her tipped glass, her cheap lipstick leaving its waxy dead dog remnants behind. As I grew more partial to Kai, I grew less so to the color of her lipstick. What had started off a pretty pink now struck me as a lifeless salmon color.

Surely, he wouldn't want to kiss a dead fish.

Andy nodded his approval and wiped his mouth with a forearm. "Decent."

Savannah wrinkled her nose. "Disgusting."

"Delicious," Kai muttered, eyes still on my face.

For a short moment, it seemed they were rating me rather

than the drinks. I crossed my arms with a slight grin, okay with that, and their assessments.

Savannah put her arm around Kai's waist, pulling him toward the vacant pool table, and I leaned over the bar next to Lewis, picking up our conversation where it had left off. Kai came back when any of them were in need of another beverage, and I stared ever so discreetly at him and his behind for the rest of the sweet, uncomplicated night.

4

SOFT RAYS OF WOMANSHINE
Kai

Faryn was all curves—her hair, her lips, her hips. She was soft even when she moved, smooth instead of jerky, and her words were tender, her gaze gentle. Savannah was suddenly hard in comparison—bony shoulders, piercing knees, and a harsh tongue.

I knew the minute we'd left the bar I had to see Faryn again today.

I knew the minute we'd left the bar I had to break it off with Savannah.

Five minutes after I knew all that—in my car on our way back to Savvy's—I'd told her we weren't right for each other. Of course, she freaked the fuck out, but whatever, I was used to that. I could hold firm. Not my fault she couldn't take no for an answer, and I ended up having to repeat, over and over, that I no longer wanted her. I wasn't coming in to spend the night. No, no, and no, not ever.

A switch had flipped inside me, and my attention was now on the blonde at the bar.

The image of Faryn leaning over it was burned into my brain—hands clasped beneath her chest and hair swept over to one side, smiling at Lewis like he had two strong hands. There weren't many people who did that, even in this town, even the ones who'd known him their whole lives.

I was consumed in a way I'd never been before, and praying to the God I hardly believed in that she would be there, I pushed open the door to Chuck's place.

Happy birthday to me, it was like they'd never left.

Faryn was grinning as Lewis told her another story— probably for the fifth time—and they quieted only to look over as I walked in. I studied her, trying to gauge her reaction. The change in her expression was subtle, but it registered. A slight upturn to her lip, a widening of her eyes. She was pleased.

As I crossed the space, she stood and swept thick curves of hair over her shoulder. I sat on the stool next to Lewis.

"Did you come for another Dark and Stormy?" she asked.

"You sound like a dealer."

When she smiled, her brown eyes creased in the most endearing of ways. I pegged her for early thirties, and I pegged her for mine.

"I'm kind of bored with all the beer orders," she said. "I

need something to challenge me."

"But you came here for easy," Lewis pointed out, like he was reminding her.

She looked at him. "You're right, Lewis, I did." And back to me. "A beer then?"

"How about a soda, and how about you join me?" I patted the stool next to mine.

"I don't know." She smiled. "Chuck runs an awfully tight ship."

"I'll run any type of ship you want me to, sugar," Chuck yelled from the tiny kitchen off the bar.

She and Lewis shared a look. How had they gotten to know each other so well in one day? Word was she'd just gotten the job. Perhaps I should give up my life and move into Chuck's too, since it seemed to be working so damn well for Lewis.

"Anything to get in your pants, I tell ya," Lewis remarked.

"Anything to get into anyone's pants, I imagine," she replied, pulling out two glasses and filling them both with soda.

"No, I think mostly yours," Lewis said. "There's a certain ray of womanshine about you."

"Why thank you, Lewis." She smiled at him. "If only I were forty years older."

"Or *I* forty years younger," he mumbled into his drink.

I smirked, ridiculously pleased that I wasn't too old or too young or too anything. Well, hopefully I wasn't too rough around the edges. But edges were pretty easy to sand down.

Faryn carried the sodas around the bar and sat next to me.

She held her glass up and I tapped it with mine. "To new friends," she suggested, in almost a whisper.

"To a certain ray of womanshine," I replied, my voice lowered as well.

Setting her drink down, she oriented herself toward me. "So, Kai."

"So, Faryn."

She tilted her head slightly, and my chest folded in on itself. I didn't recognize this feeling—the suspension in my gut, rapt for her, for what she might do or say next, her slightest movement, a tilt of her head. I wanted to be witness to it all.

I turned the glass with my fingers, round and round, and ignored the music, the rattle of pans in the kitchen, the slow beat of the ceiling fan, all so I could better focus on her.

With a raised brow, she tapped the pads of her fingertips along the worn wooden bar. "So, Savannah?"

"We're finished."

She straightened and leaned back, a naughty grin on her face. "Did you break up at the pool table last night?"

Pretty sure she was referring to when Savannah about straddled me and tried to stuff her hand down my pants.

Shit. Leave it to Savannah to ruin the mood, even when she wasn't here. I rubbed my face with one hand. "I'm sorry about that. That's just Savannah for you."

Lewis threw up an "Amen" behind me.

"As soon as we left, I broke it off."

"It's none of my business, Kai." She opened a straw and placed it in her soda, then slid it to her for a drink. "I was just teasing you, really."

"By all means," I said, "tease me." Her laughter even, that was soft too. "Do you have a boyfriend, Faryn?" I couldn't wait, I couldn't play games. I wanted her and I wanted her immediately.

She took her time with the answer, going for more soda before responding. Teasing me, as I'd asked.

I shouldn't have; it was excruciating.

Finally, Lewis stepped in. "She ain't got no one official, Kai Allen, but I'd watch yer back. I done think she got herself many a suitor last night."

I wanted to tell her that she'd sure as hell gotten me, but decided I needed to rein it in. I was all about laying it on thick, the charm, and results generally came quickly. But I'd been thinking lately about what it might be like, to be a respectable type.

If that's who I wanted her to see me as, then that's who I needed to be.

"Anyone spark your interest?" I asked.

"You mean, besides you?" she replied, again with that soft tilt of her head.

I had no control over the corners of my mouth, as they pulled up my lips with satisfaction. "Yes. Do I have any competition?"

Setting an elbow on the bar, she leaned her cheek against her hand to look past me. "Just Lewis there."

I felt like a damn romantic, for fuck's sake. What in the world had gotten into me? "Where in the world did you come from?" I asked, shaking my head.

She dropped her elbow and scooted an inch closer to me until our knees almost touched. "What do you do, Kai?"

"I run the grocery store."

"That seems like a big job."

For a punk such as myself? This seemed to be her insinuation. But I hadn't been a punk for a while now. Anyway, I was coming to think I'd damn well be whatever she wanted me to be.

And let me tell you what kind of colossal change that was.

"His dad owns the joint," Lewis broke in.

"Thanks a lot, Lewis," I muttered, bristling at the mention of my asshole father.

He slapped me on the back with his shorter-than-average appendage, and I kept focused on Faryn for her reaction. I couldn't decipher it.

"It's still a big job," she said. "Do you like it? The pressure?"

"I like it a lot actually. Resisted at first, seeing it's my dad's and all, but construction can get old." Construction had proven a good release for my anger, but she didn't need to know that. If I was going to be respectable, that meant no uncontrollable rage. "And when he started to slow down, well, it is a good gig. Bottom line is I like going to work in the morning."

Though tomorrow, I might not feel that way. I might rather come here and sit on this stool with Lewis.

"What do you do?" I asked. She swept her arms around with a smile, but I shook my head. "What'd you do before this?"

She pressed her lips tight before responding. "A little of everything. Whatever was needed."

Again, I tried to read her expression, but she wasn't as thinly veiled as the women I was used to. Or maybe it was just that I hadn't known her my whole life. "At least tell me where you're from."

She frowned, and I immediately wanted to take it back. In fact, I almost did. But then she replied, "A bigger place than this."

Everywhere was bigger than this, but that was fine. I didn't need to know. I understood what it was like to have a past, and to want to shed it. I was all about living in the present.

"Okay, let me try another angle. Are you hungry? Can I buy you lunch?"

"I don't eat here," she replied. "The food will kill you."

"Hey, now," Chuck protested, as he walked past her. He grabbed his junk and gave it a violent lift. "This is what'll kill you." Continuing around the bar, he headed past me and Lewis, settling into his spot at the other end, against the wall.

I leaned forward until my face was close to hers. "He's friskier than your average bear," I whispered.

She leaned forward the rest of the way, until her lips brushed my ear. "Leon already warned me," she whispered back. "And Lewis here."

I shook my head as we straightened in our chairs. "Lewis, if you weren't forty years my senior, I might have to take you out back and kick the shit outta you."

He patted my shoulder again. "I'd welcome that, if it

meant I lost forty years."

"Do you need another drink, Lewis?" Faryn asked.

In my insolent infatuation, I wanted nothing more than to block her gaze. I'd have to get this under control by the next time I saw her, if I wanted to appear smooth and steady and respectable.

"Nah," he replied. "I can wait. You finish your date, little lady."

"This isn't a date, Lewis. We're just having a drink. Besides, I think my break is over." She stood and made her way back around.

What did that mean exactly? Was she done with me? Had I failed? Was she requesting a real date? I'd give her a real date. Hell, I'd build her a house. I'd give her the world if I had anything to say about it.

Seriously, what had gotten into me?

We watched her for awhile, as she made Lewis another drink and wiped down the bar.

"So, where *do* you eat?" I asked, my lunch request coming back to me.

She shrugged. "Not here."

Chuck waved his hand at her and went back to the paper.

"Sorry, Chuck, but maybe you should try a grill for once, instead of throwing everything into that fryer." She leaned over the counter. "Do you realize he has fried cookies and candy bars on the menu?"

I nodded, wanting to put my hands on either side of her face and keep her there, press my lips to hers, taste her and drink her in. "They're actually pretty good," I said.

Lewis nodded, and a deep "Mmm-hmmm," emitted from his throat.

"They'll kill you," she stated.

Chuck did it again with his crotch. "This is what'll kill you."

Faryn sighed. I imagined she was glad for Lewis, super-glued to his chair like he was, or it would be a much more awkward working environment.

"I'm not kidding," I pressed. "Have you eaten?"

She smiled. "Yes, before I came in."

"What time do you get off?" I asked.

"I'm here until close," she replied. "I'm all Chuck's got."

He looked up when she said his name and licked his lips. I wanted to fucking punch his lights out. "So you'll need dinner at some point?"

"I'll probably walk home for dinner," she said.

She wasn't being coy. Was I being pushy? I probably shouldn't ask where she lived, if I could walk with her, eat with her. I probably should get a hold of my damn self. "Can I take you out for real sometime?"

"As opposed to for pretend?" She handed me a kind of grin that made my insides growl.

I waited for more, but when she offered nothing, I hung my head in defeat. I would come in tomorrow and ask again, and the next day and the next, until she agreed.

Which again, was not like me. A no was a no, and I generally moved along until I got an easy yes.

She slid her hand onto mine, which was settled palm down next to my empty glass. I looked up.

"I'd love to, Kai." Low, but not a whisper. Gentle and tender and promising, in one tone. It snared all of me, like a compass attracted to the north and unable to look in any other direction. Had this been what I'd been chasing my whole life?

"Yeah?" As if I couldn't quite believe it. When had I ever been so uncertain with a woman that I needed confirmation not once but twice?

"Yeah." She removed her hand and turned to organize the bottles on the back wall.

I looked over at Lewis.

"She has to be doing something most of the time," he informed me.

I watched for a while, wondering if I should go. It would be pathetic to sit here all day, staring at her. But if I left, she might hear my bike, which suddenly felt too flashy, too loud, too obnoxious, and too punk.

I was responsible, respectable—this was my new mantra. Could I trade in my bike? I didn't think I could. But when she turned and smiled at me, I thought I just might.

Hell, I needed to get out of here before I did something really stupid.

Laying a ten on the bar for our sodas, I stood.

"Leaving so soon?" she asked.

I patted the raised wood edge, reconsidering. But I was cool, restrained. Then, "When can I see you again?" blurted out of me.

"I'm off tomorrow, thought maybe I'd do a little grocery shopping."

"So that means you're off tomorrow night? And I could

take you to dinner?"

She nodded.

"Can I pick you up at your place, or would you rather meet me here?"

"You can pick me up at my place," she said. "It's right across the street. Upper left."

"Seven o'clock?"

She put her hands behind her back, resting them between her bottom and the shelving. "I'll be waiting."

Those being some damn fine words for her to leave me with, I nodded and left, pausing for a moment once I hit the sidewalk. The sun was harsh after the lighting in the bar, illuminating all the ways I wasn't good enough for her, all the ways in which I was a worthless human being.

But she gave me hope, and I would hold onto that until someone ripped it from my cold, dead hands. Because it felt like a gift I'd been waiting for my whole life.

I shook my head of it and forced my feet to move. I mean, honestly, what the hell was going on with me?

5

INSANITY

Faryn

After Kai left, I could hardly concentrate on work. Not that there was much to concentrate on.

Sunday evening was slow, and the uncomplicated life I'd been looking for was actually rather boring. This, I knew, would only make it more difficult for me to stay away from him.

"Hey, earth to Faryn," Chuck said, bumping into me with his hip as he passed by. He pretty much let me do all the work—aside from cooking—while he sat at the other end of the bar and observed, usually with his face in a paper or magazine. Oddly, it wasn't just the car and truck periodicals he went for, but also "Vanity Fair" and tabloids. Chuck was a well-rounded individual.

"I'm sorry." I shook my head to clear it and focused back on the three men in front of me: Lewis, Leon, and a man everyone called Gervais. "What was that?"

"Have you noticed anything funny in your new place?" Gervais repeated loudly. Not because I hadn't heard him the first time. The man, it seemed, did everything loudly.

"Funny how?"

"Funny like a ghost living with you."

Leon huffed. "Matthew wasn't like what everyone said." Matthew, the previous tenant, had taken off without notice and left his furniture behind.

"What did everyone say?" I asked.

"Everyone said he was a medium," Gervais boomed out. "Said he brought dead people back to life. Said there was a whole buttload of people livin' up there with him, so he didn't get lonely."

"It couldn't have been too many people," I commented, "if they could fit up a butt."

Lewis hooted at the jab his competition had taken. Gervais was as much of a storyteller as Lewis, only Lewis had confided Gervais was full up on pure bullshit.

Gervais was twenty years younger than Lewis, had a full head of hair and two hands. Not to mention he drew more attention with the volume he spoke.

I preferred Lewis.

"Don't listen to nothin', Faryn," Leon said. "None of it's true."

"I don't know, Leon. It does seem like someone keeps

shutting all the doors I leave open." It was an odd thing, not that I'd ever believed in ghosts.

"See?!" Gervais snapped his fingers. "Matthew died at the hand a one o' them spirits, and now they're comin' after you!"

Lewis spun his glass around. "*If* he died in that 'partment, it wasn't no spirit. It was murder or suicide."

"The place leans, Faryn," Leon said, more viciously now. Vicious for him, anyway, which was the normal cadence and strength of an average person. "If doors are shutting, it's because the house leans 'em that way. And Matthew didn't die in that apartment. He didn't die at all. If he'd a died,"—he glanced back and forth between the two men next to him—"would he've packed up all his clothes and stuff and taken them with him? No. That all woulda been left. Short notice, sure, but no funny business." Lewis opened his mouth, but Leon wasn't finished. "Matthew was a nice boy. I never much liked it when everybody started talking about him."

"That's because they started talking about you *in* him." Gervais snickered.

Leon, of course, remained calm. "I fucked your wife twenty years ago. Best you remember I could probably do it again." He glanced at me with his hound dog eyes, averting them immediately. "Sorry, Faryn. I shouldn'ta said that in front of a lady."

"That's all right, Leon. You ever need proof again, you just tell them about last night." I winked at him, and Gervais scoffed.

"Aw, hell. I don't need proof," Leon replied. "Who cares what I do? It ain't like anybody comin' over to visit me anyway."

"Philip comes over to visit you," I said with a grin.

"That *Philp* rides up my ass sideways," Leon muttered. "What's he got to be so happy about anyway?"

"Well, what you got to be so miserable about?" Gervais asked, elbowing him.

Leon didn't answer, and Lewis shook his head. "You kids just don't get it."

I grinned at Chuck, who'd glanced up to roll his eyes. I'd heard that a lot in the last twenty-four hours. I could only imagine how often Chuck had heard it in the many years before I'd shown up.

But we didn't get a chance to ask him what we didn't get, because Savannah barged through the door like the devil with her head cut off.

Face twisted like licorice, she slammed her body against the end of the bar, next to Lewis. With a hand on her hip, she opened her scarlet-trimmed mouth. "Who the *hell* do you think you are, missy? We don't go around stealing other people's boyfriends in this town!"

Lewis snorted. "You sure do, Savannah. You ain't makin' any sense."

"Oh, shut your wrinkled pie hole, ya old man."

This condescension toward him flipped my switch. "I'd watch your mouth, Savannah. We don't take kindly to assholes around here."

Lewis, Leon, and Chuck all looked at me, but I didn't care if she was a customer. It was uncalled for.

"Who you callin' an asshole? I bet your skanky ass slept

with him already. You're a slut!" She pointed at me, stabbing the air between us and defiling my personal space.

I strode around the bar. She tilted on her heels and stumbled backward. I walked her all the way to the door, which she scrambled to open, and as she stepped out, I warned her, "Don't come in here like that again. Don't speak to Lewis like that, and do not think for one second you intimidate me. You have no idea what real intimidation entails."

Slamming the door was a comical move, due to its hefty weight and the resistance from the easy close attachment up top. But I tried anyway. It turned into a shoving match, and after three attempts, it finally slid into place.

"I'll *kill* you!" she squealed from outside, from under the window. "I'll kill you so fast, you mess with Kai!"

So I pulled at the knob, ready to head out there and dare her, but as soon as she heard the door's familiar squeak, her shoes clacked away down the sidewalk.

Stalking back to the bar, I closed my eyes to rein in the bucking mustang, the part of me that wanted to chase her down and give her more of my mind. Opening them a good few moments later, after I'd collected myself and regained my calm—or maybe I should say collected my calm and regained myself—I looked sweetly at the three men in front of me. "Sorry, boys." And to my boss, "Sorry, Chuck."

"Don't mind us," Gervais said.

"Shit, that was hot." Chuck shook his newspaper out. "You do that whenever you want. I had no idea I'd hired a bouncer."

Leon turned to Lewis. "Why can't we all just get along?"

Lewis lifted his glass in response. "You, my friend," he paused, "just might get it." They toasted to that and took long drinks while Gervais pouted for being left out.

I needed another moment. So I took off, without a backward glance, for the bathroom.

6

CONFRONTATION

Faryn

After Savannah showed up, I wasn't so sure about getting involved with Kai. This meant I was dreading what should have been a fun shopping trip. But I needed groceries, there was no way around that, and maybe it was better to break the news to him before he appeared on my doorstep.

Grabbing my keys and wallet, I started down the steps in my favorite dress, one that skimmed my feet and bared my shoulders. The sunshine was as brilliant as it had seemed from inside my apartment, and I stopped before getting in the car to tilt my face up and soak it in.

There was nothing like the renewal of sunlight after a long gray season, not to mention the green grass and flower buds that revived the world from destitution. Spring recharged me like not much else, and the restlessness deep in my core was soothed and purring, soaking up the rays that streamed in through the windows of my soul.

With a sigh, I hopped in my SUV and started the engine. The music blasted loud, startling me, and I punched it off. I would enjoy a quiet ride across town today.

It was a short drive, like everything here, and as I crossed the parking lot on foot, this first time after learning the store was his domain, I started to sweat. The last thing I wanted was to tell him tonight was off, when I so very much wanted it to be on.

Before grabbing a cart, I wandered around, looking for him. I needed to rip this bandage off before I lost my determination, and as I peeked around aisles and studied the doors behind the service counter, I had to keep reminding myself Savannah had definitely brought a swift kick of complicated to my thus far uncomplicated life here.

No sign of him. Struggling with my disappointment, I had to remind myself it was a business call, a cancellation.

Yanking a cart from the line, I plodded into the produce department.

It was a really nice store, clean and well-kept. The displays were neat and appealing to the eye, sort of like Kai himself.

Ugh, you'd think I'd never met a man before.

I grabbed a bunch of bananas, a box of clementines, and a bag of grapes. Lettuce and cucumbers and carrots next, a few potatoes, onions, garlic. Then I headed for the meat department, where he found me.

I couldn't help but smile, no matter what I was here for, as he looked so completely different than he had at the bar. The misfit was hidden, gone inside a pair of black suit pants and a pinstripe button down shirt. Top button unbuttoned, and no tie, lent him just the right amount of relaxed.

He grinned widely, and it tore down the rest of his bad boy persona. "You're all dressed up," he said.

I looked down at my dress. "Oh, well, jeans seem to fit at Chuck's more than this kind of getup." Meeting his gaze again, I added, "I guess I dress down for work. And you—you clean up quite well."

His smile faltered. "You didn't like the yesterday me?"

I tilted my head. "If I didn't, would I have said yes to our date tonight?" Ooh, but that didn't sound like I was breaking it off. Running my fingers down my face, I composed myself. "Listen, I don't think I can make it tonight."

His brow furrowed.

"I'm really sorry, Kai, I am, and I really like you, that's probably obvious. I just, I need my life to stay uncomplicated right now, okay?"

"But I'm not complicated. I've never been complicated."

I danced my fingers along the cart and watched them as they went. Did I tell him about Savannah, or would that only make it harder for him to let me walk away? Who was I kidding? He was obviously a playboy. He didn't need me, and I didn't need a lover. I looked back to him and threw it out there. "Maybe you're not, but Savannah is."

"I told you." He took a small step toward me. "I broke up with her."

"I know, but she isn't ready to let you go." Turning to the

poultry case, I grabbed a package of chicken breasts. His hand landed on my shoulder, gentle but firm, and he urged me back around.

"How do you even know that?" His eyes searched mine, looking for an answer, a truth, a way back into our date. I wanted one, too.

"It doesn't matter, Kai. I'm sorry."

"It does matter. We were together for maybe three months. She has no claim on me."

We studied each other, and I watched the lines in his face. He seemed to have the same sort of duplicity I often wondered at in myself. Good, upstanding citizen, responsible and capable, yet at the same time a wild, restless mustang needing release and constant supervision.

He was perfect. He might understand me.

"She came into Chuck's last night," I admitted, "screaming bloody murder."

"She what?" His jaw clenched, unclenched, clenched again.

"It's fine. It wasn't a big deal." I looked down at his shoes, a nice pair, stylish even, and shrugged. "It's not like I can't understand why she'd be upset."

He took another step toward me and lifted my chin up with his hand. I thought he might kiss me, but instead, he held our faces inches apart. "Please let me take you out tonight, Faryn. I've never wanted anything more. I know that sounds ridiculous, but it's true. And Savannah doesn't matter. She doesn't. She can't. She's nothing."

It was too intense. I closed my eyes for some reprieve, but his scent lingered, as did his touch on my chin. Then that was gone, and all of me at once wanted to reach out to him and hold on tight for safekeeping.

I didn't want Savannah to matter, of course, and it was no secret that all relationships were somewhat complicated. Maybe she would go away now. Maybe last night was all she had in her. Besides, three months was nothing, considering we weren't in junior high.

As I was surrendering to these rationalizations, I felt him slipping away and opened my eyes in protest.

He'd reached surrender also, but from the other side. If I didn't open my mouth soon, he'd be halfway across the store and out of sight.

"Okay," I said, but it came out a whisper.

He did a one-eighty, facial muscles poised just so, gaze sliding back into mine.

"Okay." I nodded, my voice stronger. "Seven o'clock."

His wide, boyish grin reappeared, and I hid mine as I grabbed for the ground turkey.

Coming back, he walked beside me a few paces. When I stopped in front of the bags of shrimp, he peeked into my cart. "Is there anything you don't eat?" he asked. "I mean, anything you don't like, that we should stay away from tonight?"

"No fried candy bars," I reminded. "It makes me ill just thinking about it."

He glanced at the produce and lean meats I'd so far collected. "Healthy eater then?"

As if it were a dare, I marched resolutely down to the dairy case and dropped a roll of chocolate chip cookie dough into the cart.

He grinned. "Fried cookie dough?"

I made a face. "No."

"Do you eat anything that's fried?"

"Of course."

"Like what?"

We kept walking, both relieved, I think, that our conversation had taken a turn for the lighthearted. "Like onion rings."

"French fries?"

I shook my head. "I prefer potato chips. Actually, better yet, Cheetos." He waved a hand toward the chip aisle. "On occasion. And fried pickles."

He raised a brow. "Fried pickles?"

"Fantastic with ranch dressing."

He nodded. "What else do you like?"

"Um…" It was oddly difficult to pull this up quickly. "Pizza, sushi, chicken pot pie-"

"I don't just mean food," he interrupted. "I mean everything."

I twisted toward him. "That could take awhile."

"I'm all ears," he replied, tone serious, but lips curled up.

Nearly blushing from such intense and wanted attention, I pulled a box of spaghetti off the shelf. Then, over the next twenty minutes, I did the best I could to answer his question.

Shopping together like that almost felt like a first date, as had sharing soda at the bar, and in the face of such sweet, seemingly inconsequential moments, I could hardly wait to see what the real night might bring.

7

BUILDING BLOCKS
Kai

The days were getting longer and the evenings warm, so I would take Faryn on a picnic. I couldn't decide if this was corny or romantic, but either way, it had probably been done a million times. There wasn't much in town I felt fit her though. Hell, there wasn't much in town, period.

We were simple—the town was simple—and she struck me as the opposite, throwing off vibes of complexity that had me scrambling to keep up.

I'd left work early, before five, in order to scout some of my favorite spots. It needed to be out of the way so Savannah wouldn't stumble on us during her evening walk, but not so far Faryn might fear for her safety, as any single woman should if they found themselves alone, away from town, on a first date.

Then I rushed home to shower and change, back to work to pick out some flowers—it was the first time I'd actually wished we had a real flower shop, as our generic bouquets suddenly seemed quite pathetic—and then over to her apartment.

I usually didn't drive my Jeep until the first snowfall, but I wasn't going to pick her up on my bike. Parking next to the little SUV I'd helped her load groceries into earlier, I stopped myself from sticking my head in the open window to see if it still smelled like her, like it had when I'd hoisted the bags in the trunk.

I wasn't aiming for creepy.

Taking the stairs two at a time, I yanked open the old wooden door that led to the hall, took the hall at a jog, and knocked on her door.

She opened it, resting the length of her body along the wood frame with a wicked smile on her face. "I thought you rode a bike."

"How'd you know that?" It wasn't like I'd been trying to keep it from her, but I didn't figure the long dress would work so well on a motorcycle, and the flowers might have lost some of their vigor in the transit. "The flowers! I have flowers. Hold up."

I ran down to get them, nearly slamming my finger in the door in my hurry, and was breathing more heavily than I'd have liked as I returned. The presentation was not nearly as smooth as I'd planned.

Taking the flowers from my outstretched hand, she buried her nose in them, rising to her tiptoes on the inhale. Her eyelids fluttered, and she turned to the kitchen. I closed the door behind me and settled in the arched doorway as she filled a simple glass vase with water and set the bouquet inside.

I'd chosen the one with the most variety, because she seemed so multi-faceted that nothing less would've met her halfway.

I had, in a few short days, become one of those idiots I'd always made fun of for being neutered. And it didn't bother me in the slightest.

Faryn put the vase on the kitchen table and stood there, admiring them, while I admired her—her back, her shoulders, the hair I wanted to sink my hands into. She had the same dress on, scoop-necked and hugging her chest enough that it didn't matter her legs were covered. Heat worked its way through me, and I tried to squeeze out thoughts of running my hands down her sides.

No sex tonight, I warned myself, even if she was willing. I wanted, instead, to savor every slow moment of her. Not recognizing myself, I shook my head. Was it just that she was new? Someone I hadn't known my entire life?

"I heard it leaving the bar," she said.

"What?" I asked, her voice shaking me from my stupor.

"I heard your bike when you left the bar." She grabbed her keys and a sweater from the table, then walked toward me. "You'll have to give me a ride sometime."

Oh, I'd give her a ride.

Damnit, I needed to back the hell up.

Slipping her hand in mine, she asked if we were ready.

I grinned down at her. "Yes, we are." Swinging open the door, I led her into the hall and down the stairs.

"Whose car is this?" she asked as I helped her inside.

"It's mine," I responded, a bit offended. Just because I had jeans and a leather jacket on didn't mean I couldn't afford two modes of transportation. I did manage a grocery store, for shit's sake.

She tilted her head as she was prone to doing. "I guess you need something to drive in the winter, huh?"

"At the first fall of snow," I agreed, regretful I'd taken any sort of tone with her.

"Well, next time I'll dress more appropriately."

"Your dress is extremely appropriate."

She laughed. "Thank you."

A few moments of silence passed before she popped on the radio and flipped through channels. She had no patience for the deejay or the commercials, or even most of the songs. Aside from one haunting voice she leaned back to enjoy, she was busy with it most of the way there.

The spot I'd picked was at the creek, next to an old bridge and surrounded mostly by park greenery. Because the creek ran through town, its bank was tended quite a ways into the country. The path faded out by the time you got to where we were, but the area was still kept neat. A few houses sat in sight but not nearby, and the town peeked through from the other side of an apple grove.

I pulled over to the side of the road and reached into the backseat for a blanket and picnic basket. Faryn got out and pulled her sweater on, leaving her keys and wallet on the passenger seat. We walked down to the edge of the stream, and while she looked around at the landscape, I laid out the blanket and knelt down to unpack our dinner.

Eventually, she settled next to me.

"Do you ever take that jacket off?" she asked.

I stopped what I was doing and shrugged.

"Are you cold?"

"No, actually I'm kind of hot."

"Take it off," she requested. "Let me pretend you might stay awhile."

So I did. "Are *you* cold?" I asked, offering it to her in case she might want another layer.

She shook her head, but took it anyway, sinking into it and wrapping her arms around her body, dipping her head to smell the scent I'd left.

My black tee suddenly seemed inappropriate for a first date, without the jacket to cover it. "I'm sorry I didn't dress nicer. You look so nice."

"Mmm, just what a girl wants to hear," she teased. "*Nice.*"

I could've thrown out any number of better adjectives here, but chose instead to put my hand to her face, cup her cheek in my palm, and lean in for a first kiss. I started gentle, but she scooted closer and placed a hand on my chest, so I went deeper.

Her fingers curled into a fist, taking the fabric of my shirt with it, and the awakening that spread to, well, not my heart, was invigorating.

I pulled away, breathless, and rubbed my thumb across her

cheek once, before dropping it back to my side. "That's how you look."

What was really sick was that I wasn't even thinking about sex here. Well, not totally.

It took her a long moment to realize she still had my shirt clasped in her hand, and her eyes widened a bit when it hit her. I grinned and she let go, pulling her arms around her again, almost childlike, to hold my jacket tight.

After setting out the last few containers of food, I poured us two glasses of wine. I'd never dated a girl who drank anything but girlie cocktails or beer, but Faryn's eyes had meandered slowly through the wine aisle at the store.

I'd never put wine to my lips, but it was made from grapes, right? So it couldn't be all bad.

Only it was. It was awful. I made a horrible face.

Faryn laughed. "You don't have to drink it, you know," she said. "*We* don't have to drink it. I don't drink very much anymore."

"Do you like it?" I asked, nodding toward her glass.

She took a sip. "Yes, it's very good wine." Resting her nose near the rim, she added, "It smells good, too. I love when it smells good."

It did, actually, have a much better scent than flavor. I put my glass down. "I'll try again later."

A small laugh burst from her, and I threw her a lazy smile. Only, then I felt cheap using it on her, as I knew how well it had worked with so many women before. But she reached out to touch my lips, so I left it there until she blushed and dropped her hand.

I passed her a napkin from the basket, then pulled out the plates.

"We don't need plates," she said. "We can just eat out of the containers, no?"

"Whatever you want."

Crossing her legs in front of her, she reached for the fruit salad and dug into it for a chunk of pineapple. Instead of placing it to her mouth though, she went for mine.

I took it, eyes on her, and she next forked a strawberry, which she ate herself, then another and a grape. When it was clear she no longer planned to feed me, I picked up the pasta salad and started eating.

"Do you have any family, Kai? Besides your dad?"

I shook my head. "My mom left us way back, not that I can blame her. My dad's a beast."

She eyed me. "You don't get along?"

"He doesn't get along with anyone," I explained. "Not just me."

"Hmm. I might like to meet him sometime."

"No, you wouldn't."

"No, I really would. Parents can reveal a lot about a person."

I shoved a large forkful of food in my mouth. There was nothing about me I wanted my dad to reveal. Similarities might exist, but they weren't what I wanted her to see. Ever.

She frowned and set the fruit salad down. "So you never see your mom? Do you know where she is?"

"I know where she is, in general, but that's about it." I continued to eat, but this didn't seem to satisfy her. So I offered up the only other nugget I had. "I used to get birthday cards once in a while."

"I'm sorry."

I shrugged with one halfhearted shoulder. That was life. I was thirty-four now. I didn't need a mother.

"Do you miss her?"

I looked over to absorb the compassion on her face. "When I was a kid I did, but I also hated her for leaving me with my dad. Eventually, I learned to suck it up. We all have problems, right?"

Ruminating on this, she pulled the shrimp cocktail tray along the blanket until it was in front of her, dipped one in the sauce, and placed it on her tongue.

Her tongue. Oh, her tongue.

I shook my head and forced myself back to the food in my hand. If she didn't eat so slow, maybe it wouldn't be so damn enticing. Savannah, skinny as she was, ate like a fiend, shoveling food into her mouth with both hands. Faryn, on the other hand, took her time, like she knew what her mouth did to me.

She smiled when she caught my glance, and I traded the pasta salad for a shrimp, which I then offered to her.

Our eyes locked as she opened her lips, and my hand lingered before I discarded the tail, allowing her time to chew and swallow before bringing my mouth to hers once again.

She tasted sweet as she worked my lips, and I imagined that even a nibble from her would carry a gentle undertone. I had never known such tenderness could drive me crazier than raw, hot lust, but it took me to a whole new level.

For fuck's sake, it was just a kiss. Yet she had me wanting to build her a house.

Savannah used to prattle on and on about the house she wanted, but I'd never before seen the allure. An apartment made so much more sense, freed up so much more time. But now, after only three days, I was ready to set up a future with this mysterious stranger in front of me. And what, exactly, was stopping me? It wasn't like Faryn needed to know she was the reason. It made perfect sense for a thirty-four-year-old to build himself a house.

Maybe I'd have to get on that.

For now, though, Faryn and food and wine. I picked up the glass again. It didn't taste much better the second time.

"I don't know if I can get used to this," I admitted.

Straightening up to take a drink of her own, she shifted back on her knees and turned my face to hers with a small hand. I sandwiched it there with my own, and when she kissed me, the taste of the liquid was still on her tongue.

I ran my hand down her arm, her side, and back up, this time under my jacket. As her warmth seeped into my palm, my insides folded.

She would, I was certain now, be the death of me. Wrapping my arms around her, I pulled us to stand, which seemed more polite than pulling her flat on the ground. I wanted to align myself to her, head to toe.

Pulling her mouth from mine, she rested her cheek against my neck, and we stood like that, intertwined, until we regained our senses.

When we did, it was beyond awkward. "Do you want to

take a walk?" I asked.

"Sure." She took my hand, and we started along the creek, toward the trees.

When we reached the apple grove, she wove among the trunks in a very crooked line, brushing her palms against them as she went. I fell behind a bit to watch.

As we came out on the other side, I stopped her. "We shouldn't go any farther."

"Why not?"

"Savannah walks the creek at night, but not past the trees."

She grinned wickedly, wrapping her arms around my waist and pressing her body against mine. In this, I expected another boiling-point kiss, but she hopped up to place her lips against the tip of my nose, then ran back under the leafy cover.

I had to readjust myself as I followed.

"So you weren't in love with Savannah?" she asked as I caught up.

"Definitely not."

"How'd you guys get together?"

"I don't really know. We just did."

"That sounds terribly romantic," she teased.

"I think she talked me into taking her home one night, and it just carried on from there."

She smirked.

"Not that I do that a lot," I asserted quickly. Okay that wasn't necessarily true. "Well, not anymore."

She sent me a look I couldn't read.

"I mean, I respect women, I do." I did. Maybe I didn't

used to, but I did now. I respected her. And I vowed not to touch her again that night to prove it.

Her look fell to laughter.

"What?" I cried. "You wouldn't want me to lie, would you?"

"No, you're right." She snickered. "An honest playboy is exactly what I'm looking for."

A pout came to my face both naturally and on purpose. "I'm a little more grown up these days, I promise." Was I? I wanted to be. "What *are* you looking for?"

She thought about this. "Truthfully, I'm not looking for anything."

"No? Do people usually leave their lives for no good reason at all?"

She stopped walking and turned to me, hands at her sides. We stood there a moment, a slight breeze carrying over us. "Only because you were honest with me," she finally said, "will I tell you that I'm searching for simplicity. For myself. I had no plans to discombobulate that with a relationship."

"Well, good thing I'm a playboy then," I cracked.

She laughed. "Yes, good thing."

Then I grew serious. "But that's not what I want with you."

"No? You want to be friends?"

I huffed out amusement as we made it back to the blanket. "Yes, quite obviously."

We crumpled down to our previous spots, and she pulled out the donuts. I knew it was dinner, but I had a weakness for donuts. As long as I'd stood in the bakery, trying to find something else, I couldn't take my eyes off them.

"It doesn't really fit, but-"

"No need to explain," she interrupted, stuffing one into my mouth. "I love donuts, too."

Crumbs fell everywhere. I shook my head at her as she fought a smirk and tried to play innocent. Any thought of revenge I might've had quickly left me though, as she collected her hair to one side, exposing her neck and completely turning me on. I imagined kissing her there, working my way up to her ear and then back, lower, and lower, peeling off that jacket, her sweater, the straps of her dress.

It was getting hotter and hotter in my head, and she was grinning, reaching out to brush the leftover icing off my cheek. I imagined her finger in my mouth. I imagined so many things in my mouth. Then her hand was back in her lap, and I had to clear my throat of the desire overwhelming me.

Someday.

Someday she would have me, someday she would *take* me, and I would take her.

I took my momentary frustration out on another donut, and as the sky began to darken, our conversation picked up speed.

In a particular lull that came a good few hours later, she smiled at me just so. Just so, that it again had me missing the exposed skin on her arms and shoulders and back, which was too far away under my coat under her sweater. Reaching out with a tentative hand, I brushed the leather and cotton off her shoulder and rubbed at the smooth curve with my thumb. She watched me as the navy of the night slowly crept up from the horizon and the stars eased into visibility above us.

I leaned over to kiss her there, refraining, but barely, from moving up to her earlobe. She dropped her head back again, how I'd been imagining it, and before I knew it, my mouth was below her collarbone, my hand inching up from her waist.

Damn. I pulled away before I hit the gold mine and lay back on the grass, froze my limbs as best I could, and stared into the never-ending skyward abyss for sanity.

She sat, legs bent and feet off to one side, her head resting on the shoulder of the arm that held her up. As my breathing slowed, she crawled over to lie down, opening my arm so she could rest inside it.

"I've had a really nice time tonight, Kai."

I bent my head to kiss hers. "Me, too."

"Can we stay here forever?"

"I'm game." There were plenty of empty lots out here to build houses on.

"Think that friend of yours would bring us food every once in a while?"

"Andy?"

"I'll call him whatever he wants me to call him, if he brings us food."

Shifting my weight, I wiggled out from under her to prop myself up on my side and rest an arm across her waist. The better to see her.

She sighed. "And there goes my pillow."

Sneaking a hand beneath her head, I tangled my fingers in

her hair and squeezed her waist tighter to my belly.

Touching, touching, touching, it was all I could think about. I bit down hard on my inner cheek until I couldn't control it anymore. Running my tongue along her lips, I nibbled at the bottom half, and she reached up to hang herself around my neck.

"I should get you home," I said, but it was garbled from inside her mouth. Hell, I was impressed I got it out at all, what with her up against me the way she was.

With a thud, she dropped off me. "You should?"

"I'm not sure how I'm going to control myself around you," I told her. "I'm thinking I need to go home and regroup, come up with a few different plans."

Her mouth curled up and two of her fingers marched up my leg, from knee to thigh. Sliding her hand under my shirt, palm flat, she ran it up the length of my chest. Coming back down slowly, from side to side, her look was a dare. Before I could figure if she was going to hit the Holy Grail or not, I caught her wrist, pulled it out from beneath my shirt, and moved it to my lips to kiss her fingers, then stood.

I gathered our mess, and she sat up, pulling her knees to her chest with a pout.

"Did I do something wrong?" I asked. Because, let's be honest, I was well used to doing things wrong.

She shook her head. "You did it absolutely right. But I'm still allowed to be disappointed, aren't I?"

I chuckled and held a hand out to help her up. "Someday I'll let you ravage me, I promise."

I'd like to think we both fell to thoughts of such a

moment, and that was why silence overtook us as we packed up the car and drove back to her place.

I walked her up to the hallway where she took off my jacket and helped me back into it. As I ran my palms down her arms, she stepped into me, her hands coming up behind to find the skin of my back. We held each other there, her cheek against my chest, and I closed my eyes. How could I have wasted so much time on so many other women when there had been something like this waiting for me all along?

She kissed me once, softly, then pushed off, saying goodbye without a word. Reluctantly, I took to the stairs, and as I crossed the lawn, I caught her watching me from her living room windows.

I imagined her there, and felt her pull, all the way home.

8

BLOODY MARY

Faryn

Kai hadn't called. Granted, it was Tuesday and he had a real job, not to mention I didn't know his schedule. Maybe grocery stores were erratic and unpredictable.

Regardless, if he didn't try to contact me in some way today, that was it. I was done. I was too old to play games. Clearly, Kai was a playboy. He'd never denied it, not really.

And as willing as I was to overlook that and see what might happen, since a lover was all I wanted—no relationships or attachments please—I still refused to be dangled by a string.

"What's on your mind, kid?" Lewis asked, swirling the liquid in his glass with the motion of his one arm.

"Kai, unfortunately," I admitted. A lot had passed between

us last night, on many levels. Or so I'd thought. But then, you could never be sure with a playboy. And, I had to remember, I didn't want something on many levels.

Lewis frowned. "Kai's been on the mind o' many a lady."

Throwing the towel down, which I'd wiped the counter with for the fourteenth time that hour, I folded my arms on the bar and leaned over it, almost resting my cheek on the smooth, lacquered wood.

"I know he's a playboy, Lewis. This is his one chance. Today." I looked into his watery eyes. "I don't need a serious relationship—that's not even what I want—I just don't want to play games."

Pulling my phone out of my back pocket, I checked for messages. Then I checked to make sure we'd exchanged phone numbers. We had. His was filed in my contacts as proof.

Irritated with myself, I shoved it back where it belonged.

The door swung open, a shard of light breaking through the musty air, and in walked Kai, Andy trailing behind. Kai's smile was tamer today, a more knowing version of the one I'd caught in the grocery store. Straightening, I took a deep breath.

Lewis chuckled. "Can't say I wasn't rootin' for him a bit."

Kai walked over, his eyes never leaving mine, and he sat on the stool next to Lewis, I relaxed and grinned.

"Hey," I whispered.

His smile grew, losing the knowledge and gaining a bit more delight. "Hey."

"You didn't text. I was starting to wonder."

Lewis snorted.

"Texting wasn't enough. I needed to see you."

Andy choked.

Kai patted the cracked seat beside him. "Dude, sit."

"Really?"

Kai frowned at him. "Yes, really."

Andy crossed his arms.

"Can I get you something, Andy?" I asked.

"If I gotta be witness to this, maybe a pitcher. No glass."

Raising an eyebrow at him, I did as he asked. Still standing, he grabbed the handle and poured the beer directly into his mouth.

The four of us—Lewis, Kai, Chuck from the other end of the bar, and I—watched him chug half of it like we were at a fraternity party. A little dribbled on his shirt, but he was mostly graceful about it. Only when he slammed it down did our attention return to our tasks at hand. That meant "Vanity Fair" for Chuck, the Dark and Stormy for Lewis, Kai for me, and me for Kai.

"Would you like something?" I asked him.

"How long do you work until?"

I glanced at the clock. "Another half hour."

"Do you have dinner plans?"

"*We* have dinner plans," Andy said.

Kai reached up with a smile to clap him on his back. "Don't you want to get to know my girl, Andy?"

I could almost hear Andy's teeth grinding from here. Okay, so I'd have to win over Kai's friends. With a smile, I began to craft the fanciest Bloody Mary I could. Why?

Because Bloody Marys were the fanciest drink I'd learned how to make. At least, I fancied them fancy, with all the accoutrements a person could pile on top. I started with lots of vodka, because if there was one thing I could read so far, it was that Andy liked his liquor. Extra Tabasco, because if there was a second thing I could read, it was that he saw himself a sturdy, manly man. The type who wouldn't pale in the face of a little heat. And every garnish I could think of: celery and olives of course, and to the kitchen for cubes of cheese, a baby pickle Chuck sliced the long way on his own burgers, and a strip of beef jerky from Chuck's personal stash.

Marching back in, triumphant, I set it before him with a smile. "For you."

"Why would you think I'd like this?" he asked, gruff more than rude.

"Dude." There was a hint of warning in Kai's voice.

"It's all right, Kai." I looked at Andy. "People, I hear, chase Bloody Marys with beer." Not to mention, I didn't say, you seem like you could use a snack for that mood.

"Bloody Marys are a girlie drink. Who you know drinks Bloody Marys?"

I'd had an affinity for Bloody Marys in a past life. In a past life before a past life, really. And I had been a girl. Nodding, I pulled it back toward me. "Okay, point taken. I'm sorry. It's just the fanciest thing I knew how to make. My best foot forward and all that, you know?"

"Darlin, ain't nobody think you got a bad foot," Chuck piped up, not looking away from his glossy pages.

Kai went for the glass, but Andy put his hand up. "I'll try

it." Sitting down, he went for the beef jerky first, letting the wet side drip into his mouth before closing his teeth around it and taking a bite. He swayed his head and nodded, then gave me an approving look.

"Kai?" I asked. "Would you like something?"

He nodded at the Bloody Mary.

I winked and got to it, adding an extra olive and cheese cube for his culinary enjoyment.

"Remember when we did Bloody Mary in the mirror?" Andy asked Kai as I set the second drink down. He slapped a hand on the bar and laughed. "The first night we ever got toasted. That stupid girlfriend of yours. All her idea, then she gets mad at us!"

"That was a long time ago."

Andy elbowed him. "Back when you were into ghosts."

I settled my hands against the bar with interest. "You had a thing for ghosts?"

"I was obsessed with them. You know, young kid, scary stuff. We'd sneak out and go graveyard hunting, that kind of thing."

Andy snickered. "Only thing calmed her down was your hand in her pants."

Chuck glanced up from his magazine. Lewis dropped his head over to stare, and Kai cleared his throat. "Maybe we don't have dinner plans, Andy."

"Aw, come on! What's stuck up your ass?" He looked at me, then back to Kai, as if I might be the exact thing stuck up his ass.

"You should come hunt the ghost at my place," I offered.

"There's no such thing," Kai said. "What are you talking about?"

"You know them rumors," Lewis said. "Matthew gettin' murdered by his spirits. That was his apartment."

"That kid was a freak," Andy muttered between sips from his Bloody Mary and gulps from his pitcher.

"Freak or not, he wasn't murdered," Kai said.

"Oh, but his spirit lingers." I dropped my voice, soft and husky. Was I going for seductive or spinning a story? It was hard to tell. "Sometimes the lights flicker, off and on, off and on. And the breeze—there's a breeze when the windows aren't even open…"

"That's faulty wiring," Andy noted.

"And drafty windows," Chuck added.

"Or spirits. I wouldn't doubt there's some nasty souls roamin' around, not willing to let go." Lewis swigged the last of his drink and nudged the glass toward me. "Long as I been around, you see enough to know that nothin's impossible."

"Mmmm. . ." I nodded. "I might need a ghost hunter to check it out sometime. Just to make sure it's safe."

Kai was still, watching me. My heart pounded while I watched him back.

"Hey, Faryn," Chuck called from down in his spot.

"Yeah?" But my eyes didn't move. Whatever this flavor of desire was, it crackled at the base of me, bubbling up like lava, and I could see the heat reflected in his eyes—not just my heat, but what was originating in him, too.

"Aren't you left-handed?"

"Yeah."

68

"You got a twin?"

I blinked Kai out of me and glanced over to Chuck. "No." No twin. Not exactly. "Why?"

"Get this." He tapped the page of his current reading material with the back of his fingertips. "There's a theory all lefties were meant to be twins. Like, in the womb they were. Even if for just a day or a week before the other faded away or whatever."

Lewis rapped his knuckles on the bar for our attention. "I seen this show where a guy went in to the ER and they found his twin inside him, like a tumor."

Making a face at the visual, I took his glass to refill it. "Lewis, when do you have time to watch TV?"

"Chuck ain't open twenty-four hours, is he? Whaddaya think I do with my mornings?"

"My dad's a leftie," Kai offered. "Maybe his twin died and took all the good with him."

"They say sometimes a twin will eat its sibling in utero," Chuck read. "Man, this shit's sick."

"Yep, my dad definitely ate his twin." Kai took a long gulp of his drink, then made a face. It wasn't as strong or spicy as Andy's, but it was strong and spicy.

Rum, beer, lime, slide. Lewis winked at me.

"They say these people have always felt they were missing something, all their lives, then they find out they were a twin in their momma. That's almost as freaky as your ghosts right there." Chuck shuddered. "Missing something your whole life? Sad way to live."

Lewis lifted his glass, as if toasting the verification of that, and I leaned back against the thin ledge of counter behind me. "That's some life you're living, Chuck, if you're not missing anything."

He winked, but not directly at me. "I'm missin' you, sugar."

Kai threw an olive at him, and Chuck caught it, pinged it back. I snatched it off where it rolled on the counter and tossed it before anything heated up. I knew enough about testosterone to see the agitation in both their eyes.

"Boys." I jerked their attention back to me, and Andy shook his head.

Chuck waved a hand in my direction. "Just go. Go on your stupid date."

"They don't got no date," Andy replied. "Kai and I, we got a, well, not a date. We got plans. Big plans. We always got big plans."

"Come with?" Kai asked, reaching a hand for mine.

I studied Andy, holding his breath in the hopes I'd say no. Rule number one was always to win over the friends and family, but maybe staying out of the way a bit would be good enough in this situation. Anyway, I'd gotten what I needed; even if Kai was playing with me, he wasn't playing games.

"Don't worry about me," I told them. "I have food prepped for dinner and a book I've been dying to finish."

Kai shook my hand, my arm swaying with the motion. "We want you to come."

Andy snorted in disagreement.

"What are you planning to do?"

"Get shitfaced," Andy supplied.

"It's a Tuesday night," I noted, wrinkling my nose at the proposition.

"You got a problem with shitfaced?" Andy asked.

Kai glared at him. "He's not serious. We're not getting shitfaced."

"Sure we are."

"There's a game on." Kai looked back to me. "But we don't have to watch it."

"Yes, we do," Andy grumbled.

"I'm good," I decided. "You guys have fun."

"Can I at least walk you home?" Kai asked.

"I'm actually a pretty experienced ghost hunter myself," I teased.

Kai let go of me and scooted his stool back to stand up. "I'm walking you home." He looked at Andy.

"I'll wait here."

I eyed them. Was this a booty call they were setting up here? It'd been awhile since I'd been that type of girl. Two lives ago, really. Was I offended? Or willing? Would that ensure he would only play with me, rather than take me seriously? Not that I wanted serious.

After folding my counter-wiping rag into a neat rectangle, I smoothed down my t-shirt and took a deep breath. It wouldn't be long before I'd have to decide.

We met up at the corner of the bar, beyond Lewis, and I threw back some goodbyes, though my mind was on what might happen next.

What I wanted to happen next.

Kai reached for my hand after the heavy door closed

behind us, and I looked down to my toes. Things had been so smooth the night before, but here, in the light of day, they felt awkward. Closing my eyes, I tried to bring back the seeping, unstoppable heat between us, the kind that moved with intent and determination for release.

As we crossed the street, I trailed a bit behind, eyes now open and feeling like the blossoms on the trees: wide and outstretched, reaching for the sun, for an element of warmth coming from another thing, hoping to be infused—needing to be infused.

Silent, we crossed the massive gravel driveway and headed up the covered stairs where darkness snuffed out some of the warmth. Light struggled through the cracks and open knots of its wooden walls, and the effect was like walking into a fairytale.

I pressed my back against the door, and Kai stopped in front of me, his hand still holding mine. "Are you...are you coming in?" I asked his chest.

He lifted my chin up. "You told me you had dinner prepped and a book to finish."

"I do."

He raised an eyebrow. "Are you a playgirl, Miss...I don't know your last name."

"Miller. Faryn Miller." I cocked my head. "And no, I'm not. But last night, you told me you were."

The heat flamed up again. I could see it in his eyes and feel it in my gut. "I'm not playing this time. I'm not going to play with you."

His words released a whimper inside me, and I was no

longer able to deny the flood of insistence that this was what I'd hoped for. Even if that was asking for things to get more complicated.

His lips on mine, his body pressing me into the door. My hands curled around his shirt on either side of his waist, his coming up to cradle my face. His tongue, reaching out for mine, tasted of tomato and Worcestershire, a reminder of a time long ago, before my parents died, back when that was my favorite drink, back when the mustang was wild.

Before I could sink fully into that—that taste, that freedom—he pulled back.

Again, I wanted to whimper. Instead, I bit down on my bottom lip.

His thumb reached over to release my flesh from my teeth, then languidly ran back and forth on my cheek. Bending to my ear, he whispered, "I'll call you before I go to sleep. And I will see you again tomorrow. And the next day. And the next."

"Good," I mumbled, burying my face in his neck and hugging him tightly, one last grasp before he left.

Good, even though the last thing I needed was a boyfriend.

SUMMER

9

SANITY

Faryn

She'd stared at me with pointy eagle eyes from her table for the past two hours. The girl was so severe it was almost painful to look at her, though maybe that was my jealousy rearing its misshapen, bulbous head.

Kai was mine now. He'd made that more than clear in the last month, and as far as I'd been able to tell, Savannah had kept her distance. Whenever she was at Chuck's, she stayed out of my way, though maybe she'd been watching me this whole time and I'd just never noticed.

She'd come in with Andy for lunch, but he'd long gone back to work. Didn't she work? And what did she want from me anyway?

What did Andy want from me? He'd had his eyes on me, too. Both of them did, as if I'd ruined their lives, and as if they'd come in to tell me about it, albeit silently.

I hadn't meant to ruin anyone's life, and Andy still had Kai on the weekends, which was surely when it mattered most. So what if I served them all night? So what if Kai snuck around the bar to hold me from behind and kiss my neck while I mixed drink after drink after drink for Lewis? They didn't hang out there because of me; they'd probably always frequented Chuck's.

Still, there was an undertow to Andy's gaze that made me uncomfortable that day, as if he'd decided something. Both of them, as if they together—Andy and Savannah—had waited long enough, and since I wasn't going away, it was time to take action.

I forced the paranoia out and focused on Lewis, on the story he was telling me. He painted pictures with words, fine tuning his verbal canvas with threads of humor, and even though the stories came again and again, I could listen all day.

Sadly, Lewis was my best friend here. Well, not so sadly, I guess. Wise old men had a lot to say about the world, a lot that resonated with me. But aside from Kai, he and Leon were the only people I talked to on a regular basis.

I missed my sister. I missed my friends. I had to pinch myself to make sure, but I'd had them once, and I wondered sometimes if this move had been a mistake.

Peace had seemed the ultimate triumph when I'd left, and though this town was peaceful, my heart was lonely. When Kai was around, that loneliness would dissipate, but when I sat here, evil eyes on me and only Lewis for companionship, I started missing the people I'd left behind.

If I wasn't careful to keep the scraps of my old life out, Lia's angry face would creep in. Was it possible to love someone so much and hate them at the same time? Was it possible to feel so responsible for someone and yet not be able to exist alongside them? Sometimes boundaries were necessary for sanity, especially when someone was...unstable. Addicted to chaos. Impetuous.

Savannah stood, shaking me from my memories, and walked over to pay her bill. As I reached for it, she called Chuck's name.

Chuck looked up from his paper. Then went back to it.

"I need to pay for my meal," Savannah snapped at him.

"That's what Faryn's for," he said, flipping the page. "I'm about to start on my crossword puzzle."

She glared at him, probably wondering whether or not it was worth the tantrum she'd have to throw in order to get him off the stool, and I held out my hand.

Whipping her head to me, she slammed the small piece of paper down between us. I picked it up and turned to key it in the register, while she threw a ten on the bar and stormed out the door.

Grimacing at my thirty-seven cent tip, not that I'd been expecting much, I finished the transaction without her.

At least it was an early night for me, and at least Kai would be coming in soon. Sundays and Mondays were the slowest, so those had become my regular days off. Tuesdays, Wednesdays, and Thursdays, business was heaviest at lunch, so I came at noon to help Chuck open and left before dinner, sometimes after, if it was especially full. Fridays and Saturdays, I worked open to close.

It was a rhythm I'd grown accustomed to, and though the scent of fried food, alcohol, and cigarettes was something I might never come to enjoy, I'd gotten used to it.

"That Savannah been giving you trouble?" Lewis asked as I settled back next to him in my normal pose.

"You'd have seen it if she were, Lewis."

"This bar is homier than my house, Faryn. Cut an old guy a break."

At least he didn't smoke. And at least Chuck kept his ashtray down at the other end, by the wall and his pile of periodicals.

Chuck stood and walked over, bending a little as he passed in front of me. "How come you never hang out by me? That's a nice view I wouldn't mind having every day."

Clasping my hands to my chest, I popped up. How could he see any cleavage when I had a t-shirt on?

Rounding the corner, he came behind me, trailing his hand along my lower back as he went. "Don't worry, doll, you're not hangin' out." As he continued on his way to the kitchen, I checked Lewis' watch. Snack time.

Lewis scowled, and I settled back down in position. I had to look anyway, best I could, to make sure. Not that it mattered at this point. If I were hanging out, the whole town had already seen it.

"You got nothing to worry about. Just 'cuz he looks at you and imagines lingerie doesn't mean you're actually showin' any."

I lifted my head up, hair in my face.

Chuck didn't touch me on a regular basis, and when he did, he was fairly polite about it. Plus, I was pretty used to him and his insinuations that we'd light his Camaro on fire if I ever gave him the chance. But it felt different today, and I needed some space. "I'm gonna run to the bathroom, okay?"

"Want me to join ya?" Chuck called from the kitchen.

I assumed that was rhetorical and made my way to the tiny hall that led out back, blaming myself for letting him get to me, and hating how it blurred my mind fuzzy.

Sitting fully clothed on the toilet, I put my head in my hands and tried to void my mind like I'd learned to do long ago in yoga.

I missed yoga and was tempted to lay myself out on the floor, *shavasana*.

Maybe when I got home.

So I sat there, my brain reaching for zen, until a knock on the door interrupted me.

"Faryn?"

My head popped up at Kai's voice, and I scrambled out of the stall. The bathroom door wouldn't release the first time, his body in the way, but the second time it did. "Is it five already?"

"Four. I came early."

"Oh." Chuck always ate beef jerky at three, which meant I'd lost an hour, but I suppose that's what good meditation could do to a person.

"They were getting worried about you," he said. "Are you

okay?"

I nodded, wrapping my arms around his waist and nuzzling my face in his neck. Kai was sweet sanity.

"Chuck bugging you again?" he asked.

"I can handle Chuck," I insisted. "It's just some days I don't have the energy."

"I can take him out back and teach him a thing or two."

I smiled at the seriousness pressed upon his face. "What are you going to teach him?"

"How to treat a lady."

"He tells me he knows how to do that already. If you know what I mean."

He raised an eyebrow. "We all know what he means."

"Can we get out of here?" I asked.

"Will he let you go?"

I smirked. "Maybe, if I make it worth his while."

Kai made a face. "As long as it doesn't involve the Camaro."

"Too bad you don't have a Camaro," I said, not serious, while eyeing the cross around his neck. How early had he left work, that he was already changed? Usually he came straight from the store on my early nights.

"I'll get one," he said.

A soft laugh fell from me. "You don't need tricks, or cars, or anything else."

"I'll get one anyway."

I pressed my fingertips on the thick metal pendant, warm from his body heat. "Camaros don't do it for me."

"No? What does?"

Staring into his dark eyes, I set my palms against his chest. "All of you," I replied, filling myself with the truth of it.

He gathered my hands in his and caught them between us, drawing me into the most transforming kiss I'd experienced in my life. His determination and fervor spread through me, healing parts that were lost and broken, forgotten and numb.

In him, I found the amnesia I'd been looking for. Who needed solitude in the face of that? He made me forget the past, the present, and the future, anchoring me instead to something timeless.

Our lips slowed, but didn't part until he tilted his head to place his forehead against mine. "Let's blow this joint," he suggested.

I removed his arms from where they'd slipped up and around me, then headed back into the bar.

"Mind if I go a bit early, Chuck? I'll refill Lewis, and you should be set for an hour or so, right?"

"Yeah, sure," he grumbled as he generally did when Kai was around.

So I mixed Lewis another, wished him a good evening, and we were on our way. Kai held my hand as we crossed the street, and I smiled as we passed his bike. I loved that he always parked it in my lot now, next to my car, and never at the bar. I loved that this insinuated him coming home with me, and that we were at the point where such insinuation wouldn't be pushy.

I broke ahead of him to run the rest of the way to the stairs, took them two at a time, fled down the hall, and unlocked the door. He usually didn't chase after me when I did this, only slightly picking up his pace, so I knew he'd catch just a glimpse of me as I ducked into my bedroom while pulling off my shirt.

Smelling like a barfly in a beer glass was not, in my mind, how I wanted Kai to remember me when he went home at night. I threw on a dress, the one I'd worn on our first date, and smiled at myself in the mirror. It held fond memories.

Kai was on my couch when I emerged, a sly smile to greet me. I plopped down next to him and touched his lips. "What's this for?"

He scooped me up and pulled me onto his lap. "For the one second show I got before you slammed the bedroom door shut."

I smirked. "I was hoping you'd seen that."

He kissed my neck in a most irritating way. Irritating in how it made every nerve in my body jump to attention. Irritating in the knowledge he could so work me and still control himself, still not rip my clothes off.

Why didn't he want to rip my clothes off? It had been long enough. He'd proven he wasn't playing me, that this was a little something more, at the very least. And, considering the way he could work a neck, I was getting real frustrated.

"So what's with the clothes?" I asked.

He came up for air. "I'm sorry?"

"You changed. You normally come straight from work."

"Oh, I had the afternoon off."

"You did?" I pouted. "You didn't tell me that."

"It was sort of last minute." His eyes twinkled. "Want me to show you?"

"Show me what?"

"Why I had this afternoon off?"

"What, you got my name tattooed on you or something?"

"No, just your face."

I studied him, not sure for a second if he was serious or not. But he couldn't be. He wasn't the biggest fan of permanent ink. He'd gotten two as a kid, one on the inside of his upper arm, which drove me bananas when I caught a glimpse of it, and the other on his ribcage. He was no longer fond of either.

Then his face broke into a grin, and I let out a relieved sigh. My face didn't need to be anywhere but on my face.

He stood, pulling us both up, and swatted my behind. "Go get some riding clothes on."

I left the door open this time, curious to see if he'd keep himself where he was or wander over for a peek, and exchanged my dress for jeans and a tank top. Stalking out of my room with a frown, I made my way to the bathroom to put my hair up.

He appeared behind me and leaned against the doorframe. "What's with the long face?"

"Oh, nothing." I sighed dramatically and reached back to orchestrate a ponytail. "Just, aren't you even a little bit enticed?" I fixed my eyes on his in the mirror and dared him with the power of a look to jump me. His expression went from casual to intense, and he wrapped his arms around my waist.

"It's enticing enough knowing you're there," he murmured, working his lips across the nape of my neck, his hands inching their way up my shirt.

I let my head fall back as his mouth went for my shoulder, and it was here, in front of my bathroom mirror, the first time he slipped a hand up under my bra.

I exhaled a soft whimper and let him touch me until I couldn't stand it anymore, until I had to turn around and meet him.

Trying to pull his shirt off, trying to pull at mine, but this forward thinking had him stopping me. Again.

"Kai," I pleaded. "We're in our thirties."

He fisted the sides of my shirt in his hands and settled his forehead against my shoulder, which inconveniently forced his body away from mine. "I wanted to show you something."

"Fine." I rolled my eyes. "But when we get there, will you take your shirt off?"

He laughed, relaxing now at least, and let go of me. "If that's what it takes."

I brushed past to the front door. He grabbed his leather jacket, which he'd left folded over a kitchen chair, and helped me into it. This way, he'd insisted the first time he'd done it, if something happened, my skin would be protected from the street. Then the spare helmet he now left in my safekeeping, a silent promise, I think, that he was not taking any other girls on sexy midnight rides, and we headed out.

It was the same route we'd taken on our first date, out by the creek, the bridge, and the grove of apple trees. We slowed to a stop maybe a quarter mile past where we'd picnicked that night, and I was greeted with a whole lot of nothing.

"This is a whole lot of nothing," I said. "Now take your shirt off."

He struggled to control a grin and did as he was told. The tattoo on his ribcage was an intricate black dragon with fierce teeth and fiercer claws, while the one on the inside of his bicep was the Om symbol. This had previously gotten us into a long discussion of yoga, which he knew nothing about.

He said Om was the sound of the breath of God, and that he'd gotten the tattoo to make up for the lack of fatherly guidance he was getting from his own single parent. It hadn't done anything, he'd added wryly, and thus he'd acted like the dragon on his side for the entirety of his twenties.

Tilting my head with an appreciative sigh, I reached out to run my hands up his chest. He saw me coming and slipped away into the field.

I followed with crossed arms. "I don't get it. Did you bring me out here to ravage me or what?"

Standing tall, he puffed up his chest a bit. "Maybe after there's a house to ravage you in."

I stumbled, in thought and in foot. "A house?"

He nodded decisively. "I'm building myself a house."

Studying him with carefully contained terror, I hoped this wasn't about me. I did not want a house. A house came with responsibility. I wasn't ready for that. I was running from that. But he hadn't said he was building *us* a house, so maybe I was overreacting.

"Aren't you happy for me?" he asked, his face dropping.

I shifted my weight to one hip and dug my toe into the ground, squinting at the sun behind him. "Of course I'm happy for you."

"You said it yourself, I'm in my thirties. Shouldn't a man in his thirties have a house?"

"If he wants one, I guess."

He took a step toward me, his smile now completely gone. "There's no pressure on you. Do you feel like this puts pressure on you?"

I shook my head as he closed the rest of the gap between us. "Of course it makes sense you'd want a house," I said. "It's just…houses demand maintenance, snow removal, lawn care. They take up time and money, and they're, well, they're complicated."

"Okay," he said, running his palms up and down my upper arms. "So I've got some work ahead of me. I'm cool with that. Besides, I've gotten a little soft since I've given up construction."

I couldn't help but smile at this and uncrossed my arms so he could continue down the length of them to my hands. "I'm sorry," I apologized. "I'm happy for you, really. We should celebrate."

Pulling me closer, he asked, "And how do you suppose we should do that?"

I kissed him where my face landed, on his bare chest, and reached my fingers into his pants, rounding them along the curve of his behind, as best I could with his darn belt on.

"There's only one thing I want to do to you right now," I admitted.

Kai brought his hands to my face and tilted it up to his. "You must stop trying to take advantage of me. I am but a sweet, innocent boy." He nibbled gently at my lip, and my stomach churned with insistence.

"Let's sleep here tonight," I suggested when he pulled his mouth from mine. "We could camp out."

"It would be our first night together," he noted.

"And a *chaste* one at that," I said, rolling my eyes.

He grinned. "Maybe not completely."

"No?" I raised an eyebrow.

Releasing my face, he grabbed my wrist and started running, tugging me back to the bike. We flew to his dad's, who I'd met for two seconds a week ago, and rummaged around in his garage for a tent.

Kai was hyper there, tense, and we got out as soon as we could.

Then we went to his apartment. He grabbed the pillows, blankets, and a flashlight, while I whipped together some sandwiches and packed a few waters in a cooler. Toilet paper, I wanted toilet paper, and we piled everything into his Jeep.

We were set up by seven and eating dinner by eight.

"I didn't bring pajamas," I said as I took my last bite.

"You won't need pajamas," he responded.

I'd been pulling for hints all night, and the flirtation had me about as worked up as I'd ever been. Well, that and his body, his face, his smile, the respect he had for me that this hadn't already happened, how special he made me feel on a constant daily basis, and the fact I was almost thirty-four and it had been a bit of a while.

My body was positively taut with anticipation, like a live, charged tightrope of wire.

I wanted to beg him to take me into that tent.

"So I'm trying to decide between a tri-level or a ranch," he said.

With a growl, I threw my sandwich toward the street. He cracked up, and I laid myself flat on my back, anchoring my need to the ground.

Huh, is that why he'd done it, back on our first date? It sort of worked.

He finished eating while humming a tune, then took his time picking up our remnants, the whole while sporting a rather charming smile on his face. Once everything was in place, he came to stand over me and offered me a hand.

I took it, and he led me inside the tent.

After zipping up the entry, he faced me. "There is one rule."

My shoulders slumped.

"Anything is allowable except intercourse. That we're saving."

They popped back up. I could live with that. I could live with everything else.

He lifted my shirt over my head, palms sliding up my sides and thumbs dragging over my bra as he went. I tried for his belt, but it was somehow impossible, and soon he put his hands over mine to still them.

"I've had this belt since I was twenty. Never wore it before you showed up, 'cuz it's nearly impossible to get off. After our first date, I figured it would come in handy, slow us down if I needed to regain some sense." He explained this as he worked it off, with a decent degree of difficulty.

"You've had a chastity belt on this whole time?" I asked, eyebrows high with amusement.

He frowned. "What else was I supposed to do?"

I laughed. "And here I thought I wasn't slutty enough for you."

He gave me one of those intense looks he pulled out from time to time. "You are perfect, Faryn. You are maddening in your perfection, and you may never understand how badly I want you. How you haven't noticed me frothing at the bit, I do not know."

I gave him a gentle, thoughtful look, as he finally managed to get himself free. "Kai, you are the sweetest, most respectable guy I have ever had the pleasure to lay hands on."

10

AN OLD-FASHIONED BBQ

Kai

I'd figured one night with Faryn would ease things and help me hold out a little longer, but instead, it had turned me into a red hot fucking poker.

Like the coals in Leon's grill, that's how I'd felt these past few days. It was Sunday, Leon was grilling, and Philip had stopped by with his sweaty-ass self to have a beer.

I swear every time that creeper saw Faryn outside, he found something he'd neglected for the last twenty years to come fix. Today he'd driven by and waved at us, just as we'd been setting up, and fifteen minutes later, he comes tooling down the street on his riding lawnmower.

Twenty more minutes and he'd finished the lawn, parked

the mower between my bike and Faryn's SUV—hint, no?—and sat down on Leon's front porch.

I wanted to kick the toothy grin off his face, the way he wouldn't stop drooling at her. And didn't his mother teach him not to stare straight into a girl's cleavage? Even I knew better than that, and I'd been a dog.

"Aw, come on now," Faryn purred. "You don't think he deserves a beer after all the work he's put in today?"

Leon was stingy as fuck with his beer, and Philip had been hounding him for twenty minutes about the cooler at his feet.

"He didn't do shit today," I grumbled. What he'd done was glue his eyes to my girlfriend. Creepy SOB.

Faryn patted my knee, then slid her hand up a bit to rest it on my thigh, which immediately threw my thoughts from other men. "Leon, can I *pay* you for a beer, for shit's sake?" I asked. "So we can stop talking about this?"

"Matthew woulda given me a beer," Philip mumbled.

With a more than average droop to his shoulders, Leon opened the treasured cooler and handed his landlord a can, turning back to the grill with a pout. The meat, at least, he wouldn't complain about sharing, because it wasn't him who'd bought it.

We had our Sunday BBQs pretty well ironed out. I brought the protein, Faryn whipped up some potato salad, and Leon brought the beer—for himself.

I tried not to drink alcohol around Faryn, as it made me more amenable to the thought of ripping her clothes off. And that was just for starters.

At Leon's nod, Faryn stood to get our plates ready. She

had on a pair of short cutoffs and a tank top, and as she leaned over for the potato salad container, Philip's eyes about bugged out of his head.

I threw my empty soda can at him, wishing it were a bottle or at the very least full. He slapped at it and looked over to me, all apologetic-like.

My ass, he was apologetic.

And if he told her one more time how great it was to see her, I swear I'd place that fat smiling cheek of his straight on the burning grid of Leon's grill.

"How long ago'd he move out?" Faryn asked.

"Matthew?" Philip, of course, jumped to respond. "A few years, I'd say."

"Really?"

"Really." He nodded.

"I wouldn't have guessed you for the cleaning type," she said, handing Philip his plate.

"I ain't," he assured.

"Well, you kept that apartment up."

"I did?"

"The place was clean when I moved in. The only thing I had to wipe down was the kitchen table."

Philip picked up his burger and pointed it at her. "That's 'cuz ghosts don't eat."

I rolled my eyes, as did Leon. "There aren't any ghosts up there," I said.

"You think ghosts kept the place clean?" Faryn seemed halfway between belief and disbelief. Or maybe it was a wanting to believe that I saw.

"I think that's a full head of baloney," Leon remarked. "If anybody's been up there, it's the kids. They always lookin' for a love shack."

"Or Chuck," I agreed.

"Or Chuck." Leon nodded, taking the initiative and grabbing his plate from Faryn.

It shook her out of whatever fog she was in, and she handed me mine. "I can't imagine Chuck would deviate from his beloved Camaro," she said.

We all grinned at this. Well, all of us but Leon, whose lip twitched. But that counted.

"How's that house comin' along, Kai?" Leon, thankfully, changed the subject.

"Oooh," Philip oozed. "That there's a nice piece a as—I mean, land you got there, Kai. Super nice piece of land."

I clenched into my burger so hard my fingers met. "I don't appreciate you calling Faryn a piece of ass, *Philp*."

"So pretty with the prairie grasses and the crick. I bet the night sky's great out there, Kai. Super great. Oh, that's a nice piece a-"

His words stumbled in the face of my glare. Leon's mouth did its twitchy smile thing—he hated Philip about as much as I did—and Faryn tilted her head at me.

"It was just a slip of the tongue, Kai," she said. "Calm down."

Shifting awkwardly in my chair, I tried to finish my burger before it resembled mush. Just had to get through this meal. We would eat, finish our drinks, and then go upstairs.

"You haven't started building already, have you?" Leon

asked.

I shook my head. "Maybe next week, I'll head over to Don's and look at some floor plans."

"I had a house once," Leon said, squinting up at the sun.

"What was it like?" Faryn asked.

"My wife made it up all nice, into a home. It was a good home." He turned his head away from us, and we grew silent, even careful in our chewing. Leon had spent his first thirty years acquiring things, only to spend the next ten losing them.

It made me appreciate the fact that I'd just begun my acquiring.

"I had a house once, too," Faryn said.

I looked at her in surprise. She smiled a sad smile at me, then stood and threw her plate into the trash Leon kept by his porch.

"I've had enough sun today, boys," she said. "I'll be upstairs, okay, Kai?"

I watched her curiously until she disappeared under the covered staircase, then turned back to my plate and to Philip, whose tongue was sticking out of his mouth, eyes where she'd just been.

"So help me, Philip, I will not hesitate to wipe your face on the blades of that lawnmower." Crumpling my plate in my hand, I threw it at him, the potato salad flying out and hitting its mark.

He wiped a chunk from his cheek before putting his hands up in surrender, and I shook my head, pointing toward the stairs. "She is no one's piece of meat, do you understand? Stop looking at her like that."

Two strange expressions came my way in response to this comment. They were used to my vicious tongue and somewhat consistent follow-through, but they were not used to my concern over the treatment of the opposite sex.

I stood, unsure if she wanted to be alone for a bit, but also unsure if I could stand Philip's sugar-coated weirdness any longer. I sent a silent apology to Leon for leaving him alone and marched up to join Faryn.

She'd left the door open an inch, and I closed it on my way in, heading directly for the kitchen in order to wash my hands. When I shut the water off, my ears picked up her sniffling.

Winding past the couch, I moved toward her room and stood in the doorway. She sat on the bed with a tissue in hand. "Hey babe, you okay?" I asked.

"I'm fine, just allergies."

"Is this about the ghost stuff? Because there aren't any ghosts."

She shook her head, but wouldn't look at me, so I stepped in and sat next to her. I pulled her chin over with my fingertip, and her watery eyes reluctantly followed. She tilted her head, a gesture she often did playfully, and when that didn't wipe away my concern, she resorted to a funny face.

I sighed and wrapped my arms around her. She didn't like talking about her past. I got that. Mine wasn't so great either, and I'd prefer she not have to hear it. I was starting over as the man I'd always wanted to be, but never thought I could. We were starting over together, and the past didn't matter.

So I didn't ask any questions.

"Can we just watch a movie?" she asked. "I don't feel like doing much else."

My face fell into her thick head of hair. "We can do whatever you want," I mumbled.

She grabbed my hand and led me to the TV, then clicked into the menu on her screen and picked the first pay-per-view title.

"Whoa, whoa, whoa," I said. "We are not watching that."

"Why not?"

"It may as well be titled 'Sex, Fucks, and Rock and Roll.'"

"It's been nominated for awards, Kai. It can't be that bad."

I took the remote from her. "It's that bad." We hadn't made it to the couch yet, and were both standing between the coffee table and the small entertainment center.

With a pout, she wrapped her arms around me. "You have the swagger of a man who wouldn't be opposed to a little 'Sex, Fucks, and Rock and Roll.'"

I gave her a look. "Rule number four: no sexy movies."

She dropped her hands with a huff. "You're going to give me a complex, I swear."

"What in the world are you talking about?"

Plopping down on the couch, she bent her legs up and hugged them to her chest. "Was I not good the other night?"

I let out a sharp laugh. "Oh Faryn, that is so not the problem."

"Then what is it, Kai?" She looked up at me, so vulnerable, eyes wide and forehead furrowed. "Why's your belt back on?"

Setting the remote on the coffee table, I sat down beside her. "The problem is how hard of a time I had not putting myself inside you."

Moments passed. The breeze blew in from the windows across the room and lifted stray strands of her hair. A car rumbled by on the street. A door slammed—a car door, from the gas station next door. All of it white noise, the only thing clear was her, sitting in front of me, this most beautiful, perfect thing.

She broke eye contact and curled her fist to her heart. "But you *are* inside me," she muttered.

"You're inside me, too." I said. Like it was a vow. A promise. A pact. "You are inside me, too." I ran my fingers down the hair at the side of her face, then grabbed her chin and pulled it up, rubbed my thumb across her lip. Her brown eyes were still glassy, a message to me on how carefully she needed to be treated and a reminder that this was who I was now, someone who treated women carefully.

With my hand still on her chin, I said, "This restraint is me trying to show you how special you are. You've made me want to be a better man, the best one I can be. I've done it wrong with every other woman I've known, and I don't want to have held out longer with them, who've meant nothing to me, than with you. But, if it bothers you that much, you can take me tonight. Now."

"That's why you're waiting?"

"The only reason."

She closed her eyes. "Well, how much longer then?"

"You can take me tonight," I repeated, dropping my hand.

"No." Her eyelids fluttered open. "I just want to know how long."

"A month and a half."

She did some silent calculating. "Ninety days total? Who made you wait three months?"

"My first time, with my first real girlfriend." I thought back on all the women since. "Heck, maybe my only real girlfriend."

"I can't believe how jealous I suddenly am." She laughed at herself. "What was this hussy's name?"

"Miranda."

"How old were you?"

"Almost fifteen."

"How old was Miranda?"

"Seventeen."

"She *was* a hussy."

"She kinda still is."

"She lives around here?"

"Of course."

"What does she do? What's she like?"

"She works the vending machines in town with her ex-husband, when she's not sleeping around."

Faryn made a face. "You better keep her away from me."

I grinned, and she eased her grip from around her legs, dropping them to a more relaxed position.

"I'm kidding," she said.

"I know," I replied.

With a head tilt, she clarified, "Sort of."

I bent forward to kiss her.

"Show me, please?" she mumbled from under my lips. "Show me how much you want me, and I'll shove you out the door before you do anything you don't want to do."

I opened my eyes as she rubbed her face against mine, nuzzling me like we were feral animals.

"Okay," I agreed. It was hard to resist.

"Okay," she whispered, pulling back to look at me.

And letting her lead our mouths, I did what she asked, showing her my desire with the work of my hands. When they'd had enough roaming, over and under and around fabric, I jerked her onto my lap. Pulling her tank off and sliding her bra straps off her shoulders, I let my fingers trail down bare skin, down to her waist, thumbs up along the inside of her thighs.

Before I knew it, I had her bra off, my shirt, clambering for my belt—

She put her hands on mine to still them. With a groan, I dropped my head back on the couch. Her palms slid lower, but over my jeans as the trusty belt had not let me down, to hold in her grasp veritable proof of my attraction for her.

I opened one eye.

Her face was not teasing, like it often was in these situations, but intense like I hadn't seen it before. She leaned forward until she was resting up against me.

"In every way but physically, you are already deep inside me." Her tone was determined, like the repetition of the thought alone wasn't enough to drive this truth into me.

I scooted forward, to the edge of the couch, and wrapped her tight in my arms. "I've never been here before. I've never known anyone like you."

She about choked me with her response, first with the

arms around my neck and second with the words out of her mouth. "I feel the same, Kai. Like you're my first, all over again, but the right way. Like we were fated. But now you have to go."

Standing, I pulled her up with me, and we walked through her small apartment. She crossed her arms over her bare chest as I pulled my shirt back on, but when I reached for the doorknob, she lightly touched my back.

The hug we shared was tight, heads close together, the silky skin of her back under my arms. When I finally let go and turned around, she pressed her body up behind me and slid both hands into my jeans, as far as they would go.

It wasn't far, thanks to the belt, but it didn't need to be.

I let out a low groan and shuddered with pleasure, while she stood on tiptoe to kiss the back of my neck.

"Someday, Kai Allen. Promise me."

"Someday soon. I promise you."

I didn't move until she chose to release me, then sped home in need of the coldest fucking shower ever.

11

A FAILED ATTEMPT

Kai

It was all I could think about, a cold shower. I peeled into my spot, flew off my bike, ran up the walk, and charged into my apartment building. The key didn't work on the first try, like it had locked the door instead of unlocked it, and I about broke it in half trying to force it.

It worked the second time, and I slammed the door behind me, making my way to the bedroom, peeling off my shirt, tossing it on the bed. I had one hand on my damn belt when I realized the lump of unmade comforter was bigger than normal.

As Savannah rose from beneath it, like a witch rising from the dead, she twirled my discarded shirt around her finger.

"Hi, lover," she cooed.

She'd never known how to talk sexy. It was supposed to be a *purr*, like a tiger, not a voice one might use with a baby.

"What are you doing here?" I snapped.

Flinging the mound onto the floor, she exposed naked angles and motioned for me to join her.

"Fat chance," I said. "How'd you get in?"

"Andy lent me his key." Struggling onto her elbows, she posed herself. "Don't you want a good time, Kai? I'm sure that wallflower of yours can't even begin to imagine the things I've done to you."

I was tempted to forcefully remove her, but she was stark fucking nude, and I didn't want to get near her with a ten foot pole. Not only because any woman besides Faryn now turned my stomach—and let me tell you, that was quite a change, the novelty of actually preferring monogamy—but because I wouldn't want to have to explain to anyone, let alone Faryn, how I accidentally brushed up against any of that.

"Get the hell out of my house, Savannah."

She sat up with a jerk. "I gave it time," she snarled. "But I am sick of waiting. You don't get to build her a house, Kai. That house is mine! You are mine! I told you I wanted that house!"

The desire Faryn left me with nursed its way to fury. "I would never have built you a house, Savannah. And I will never sleep with you again. So *get out*." My arm threw itself toward the front door, the way I wanted to throw her out the damn window.

She lay back on my mattress, arms at her sides and legs

together. "Make me," she dared, tightening her body into the shape of a two by four. Or really, a one by five.

"You don't want me to make you," I warned.

She kissed the air in my direction. "Oh, but I do, lover."

"Stop calling me that."

"Lover, lover, lover," she taunted.

And that was fucking it. I untucked the fitted sheet, threw her clothes on top of her and collected the corners in my hand. She watched me but didn't move.

As carefully as I could, I eased her body off the bed, ignoring the thunk and the cry, and dragged her into the hall.

"Fine!" she yelled. "Fine, just stop."

Letting go of the sheet, I took a few steps back, looking away so she had some privacy to dress. But the next thing I knew, she was sliding up against me. I shoved her away from my bare chest and into the wall.

Frankly, I didn't think I'd pushed her that hard, but skin against skin had freaked me the fuck out. She landed with an oomph, only to place her palms against the wall and wiggle in a way I'm sure she thought was seductive.

I marched into my room, her footsteps quick behind me, and grabbed another shirt out of my closet, not sure where she'd flung my first one. I'd find it later. Pulling it on, I left to find Andy. I'd make him deal with her. Giving her my damn key. What the hell was he thinking?

I had to yank him from his precious TV and scattered beer cans and railed on him the whole way back to my place. Then I paced in the hall while he cleaned up the mess, trying to drown out Savannah's wailing with fingers in my ears.

Eventually, Andy emerged with her hair in his fist.

I winced, but couldn't really blame him, as she was flailing her skinny appendages in every direction. I guessed by the mismatched buttons that he'd had to forcefully dress her, and I backed up against the wall to let them by.

This was some crazy shit.

They fought each other in the backseat as I sped her home, and I waited in the Jeep while Andy deposited her inside. Then I scolded him again for handing over my key to a crazy ex-girlfriend.

He simply slapped me on the back and suggested we get a beer.

"I'm seriously pissed at you right now," I reminded him.

"Naw, don't be like that. She told me she left some stuff at your place and wanted to sneak in while you weren't home to get it."

He couldn't really be that stupid, could he? "When has she ever told the truth?"

Bristling, he grumbled, "At least she's the same person she was two months ago."

I glanced over at him, suddenly aware that he'd done this because he was pissed at me. I'd left him behind, and if there was one thing Andy didn't like, it was being left behind. "You knew what she was doing. Maybe she didn't tell you, but you knew."

With a scowl, he looked out the window. "I guess I just don't care anymore."

"Don't care? That's great, Andy. Two months, I'm a little preoccupied, and it wipes out twenty years? Fuck you."

"Okay, okay, I'm sorry." He looked down at his lap. "Sure you don't want to get a beer with me?"

I sighed. "I don't know, Andy. It's almost nine."

"Nine?" He shook his head at me. "We used to stay out 'til bar time almost every night of the week."

"Maybe when we were twenty."

"It ain't about our age, Kai." His tone had turned again, colder. "You just went and got all distinguishable for a girl."

"Distinguished," I corrected.

"Whatever." He glared at the street in front of us.

I pounded my head back against the seat and weighed my options. It would be a quiet night at the bar, and it had been a rough rollercoaster of a day. I wasn't sure I'd be able to get to sleep soon anyway; desire and fury were not effective sedatives. Fine, one beer. Maybe two.

Andy grinned when he realized where we were going, and before I was even in park, he jumped out of the car with a whoop.

Lewis wasn't there, for once, but I avoided his stool anyway, out of respect. Andy hopped up on the other side of me and asked Chuck for a pitcher.

"I'll have a Dark and Stormy, actually," I said.

Andy gave me a look. "Pussy."

I rolled my eyes. "Fine."

Chuck filled a pitcher and slammed two glasses on the bar with a grunt.

I looked at him funny, but instead of telling me what his problem was, he fled to the kitchen to snarf down a bag of potato chips. I could hear him chomping from where I sat.

It'd been a while since I had a beer, and I was surprised how good it tasted. So good I drained the first glass all at once.

Andy nodded with a grin. "Thatta boy. Now tell me your problems."

I snorted. We'd never told each other our problems. Guys like us didn't do problems.

"Wanna hear mine?" he asked when I didn't take the bait.

"Sure."

"See, this girl came into town a few months ago, and she done stole my best friend right out from under me." He looked into his beer. "Now I gotta drink all by myself at home. Kinda sad, right? We used to do all this fun stuff, back in the day."

"So it wasn't that you didn't care," I noted. "It's that you wanted me back with Savannah."

He shrugged. "You've never said no to a piece a ass. I figured you'd enjoy her. Naked lady, stretched out in your bed. I was thinkin' like it was a gift, from me to you." He shook his head. "Man, I wouldn't a turned her down."

"Then maybe you should ask her out."

He frowned. "She only got eyes for you. Anybody can see that."

I studied him, till it dawned on me. "You like her, don't you? Shit, you shoulda told me. I woulda handed her over ages ago."

He placed his forehead on the rim of his glass. "I get that Faryn's beautiful, Kai. There ain't no denying that. But she doesn't live like we do. Savannah lives like we do."

"How's that?" I wondered.

"Hard and fast."

I swirled the amber liquid around in my glass. It was my second beer, and almost empty already. How'd that happen?

Andy noticed this also and refilled it.

"A person can't live that way forever," I said. "That's how you burn out. You wanna end up like Lewis someday?"

"What's so bad about Lewis?" he asked, disgruntled.

"Nothing. I just, I want more. I want a house and a family. I want what I didn't have." I'd also begun to think I might not totally suck at being a dad, but I wasn't going to tell him that. He was unhappy enough with me as it was.

Andy shook his head. "I never thought you, of all people, would change for a chick."

"I didn't change *for* her, Andy. I changed for me. Just because she inspired it doesn't mean it's her fault. Don't blame her."

We sat in silence after that, draining our beers, and even though I knew I shouldn't, I poured myself a fourth.

It had been that kind of night.

12

NEARLY DESTROYED

Faryn

I woke to birds chirping, sun streaming in through the blinds, and the memory of Kai pressing down an achingly pleasant way on my heart.

Things with him—and he himself—only got better and better, feeding a strength in me I'd hoped many years for, a strength I hadn't been sure I'd ever attain.

My mind was clear, and the strong desire for a man purred along my skin. I'd had relationships before, of course, and knew this temptation would fizzle a bit eventually, burning itself out into a less intoxicating but more substantial mixture of goodness that could actually be kept up long-term, but I'd enjoy it for what it did for me today. And what he would do for me in another month or so.

With an uncontained grin, I took a shower, got ready, and enjoyed a long cup of coffee, all amidst thoughts of Kai. Pacing my apartment until noon, I replaced all the little things that had moved during the night.

I was starting to wonder about these ghosts. I mean, it could've been me who put the tape on the right side of the desk when it normally sat next to the stapler on the left, but I didn't remember using it in the first place, so why would I move it? Whatever, Matthew's spirits didn't really scare me. Or maybe I should say, until I woke up to my knives displaced, his spirits wouldn't scare me.

When Chuck opened up, I headed across the street. My plan was to grab the cash due me, head over to the grocery store, and treat Kai to lunch. It would be a surprise.

Pulling open the door to the building I now knew so well, I was greeted by strange faces on the people who were no longer very strange to me.

"What's up?" I asked as Lewis ducked his face into his drink. Walking behind the bar, I looked pointedly at Chuck. "Something wrong?"

With nervous hands, he opened the till and started counting out my paycheck.

I tilted my head. "Chuck?"

"Yeah?" But he wouldn't look at me.

"You should tell her," Lewis piped up.

"Tell me what?" I glanced to him. "Want me to mix you a drink before I go?" It was standing lore now that my Dark and Stormys had a special something about them Chuck's didn't.

In my opinion, it was just one of those things they talked up, in order to have something to do, which then took on a life of its own. But I played along.

Lewis waved his hand at me, eyes on my boss. "If you don't tell her, I will," he said.

"Tell me what?" Was I going to lose my job? I mean, it was clear Chuck didn't really need help, he just liked having it. Had I done something? Had I left early too often? I didn't leave early unless Kai came in and the place was deserted, but Chuck had a growing problem with Kai. Would he fire me over jealousy?

Maybe.

"Chuck, please?" Concern was now evident in my voice.

He looked up from the wad of cash in his hand. I had never before pleaded with him or wanted something from him in this way. I imagined he was quite enjoying it.

"I don't think you should keep seeing Kai is all." He shoved his hand at my stomach, where I caught the money he was handing over and pried it from his fingers.

Placing the bills in my wallet, I readied myself for him to regale me with reasons he was a better fit—for my body. He'd done this before. Recalling those times with irritation, I clipped out a "Why not?"

"Can't you just take my word for it?" he asked, clearly wounded by my tone.

I gave him a look. How could I bare the obvious fact that he had a thing for me? He gave me sorry excuses day in and day out about why he was better than Kai, and sometimes acted like a child because of it. That was why I couldn't take his word for it.

But he was my boss, so I couldn't say this and expose his vulnerability. I'd been a boss once too, and had my subordinates spoken to me inappropriately, for whatever reason, I would've rebuked them. That was how it worked, the chain of command. It might suck, but it was life.

Chuck took a step back. "I'm trying to protect you, Faryn."

"It's not your job to protect me, Chuck. You're just my boss." I winced at how painful this might sound to him, but perhaps he needed to hear it.

Lewis slammed his glass down on the bar, as if trying to shake us from this particular trajectory of conversation. We both glanced at him and then turned back to each other.

Chuck crossed his arms. "I thought we were friends."

"Fine!" Could I help being exasperated right now? No, I didn't think I could. "But friends tell each other what's going on."

He frowned. "You don't think we're friends?"

"Chuck! You're my employer; it's a hazy line. You want to be friends, fine. We're friends."

He sneered, then spit his spite out at me. "Kai slept with Savannah last night, okay? You happy now?"

I tilted my head, quite doubtful and a tad angry. "How would you even know that?" Was he resorting to lies now?

"He came in after, to get plastered."

I looked to Lewis, who shrugged. "I wasn't here at the time," he said.

"What time?" I asked, daring Chuck to come up with an

hour I could directly refute. Kai had been with me until eight.

"A little after nine." He looked at his feet. Ultimately, Chuck was a softie, lashing out only in short bursts when cornered. Already he regretted what he'd said, no matter how I'd just wounded him.

While I glanced again at Lewis, my stomach turned.

"I know, it was an early night," he admitted.

I crossed my arms. "And he told you he slept with Savannah?"

"No." Chuck looked up. "But I heard him talking to Andy about it."

"What'd he actually say?" I didn't believe it of him, of the Kai I knew, but he had left awfully hot and bothered. Maybe this was part of his plan, to hold out by relieving himself elsewhere, the one tactic he hadn't explained to me. Maybe he wouldn't think it counted, if he'd already slept with her before.

Chuck ran his hand through his hair. "They were talking about why Andy gave Savannah Kai's key, and a naked lady stretched out in Kai's bed, and how Kai never said no to a piece of ass. Then Kai got toasted, which is more remorse than I've seen out of him before, so at least there's that."

My hands shook, and I stuffed them into my armpits so no one would notice.

Could it possibly be true? And what would I do if it were?

I considered fleeing to the bathroom, but stillness seemed my best option. If I moved, I might shatter. Only this left Chuck to continue prattling on.

"You know, this shouldn't be a surprise. I warned you he

was a ladies' man. I know I might look like one, but I'm not. He is, through and through, and the number of women he's left in his path is astounding. He's hardly ever been faithful, he's all about sex, and he treats his girlfriends like shit."

Clamping my teeth down on my lip didn't keep my eyes from tearing, and Chuck noticed this. He reached out to hug me. I jerked back. "He doesn't treat me like shit," I said, my voice weak like I hadn't heard it in a long time.

"He doesn't," Lewis spoke up. "I think he might love you, actually."

I turned to him, grateful. "I think he might, too."

He nodded. "Does seem that way."

"Do you think he did it?" I asked him.

Lewis didn't answer right away. Then, "He's a different Kai than the one he was in his twenties, and I don't take too strongly to hearsay."

I nodded at the hope he handed me, packaged inside a little burst of energy I desperately needed, and turned to run quickly into the truth, before I lost my nerve.

13

Deterred

Faryn

I flung open the door to his office, hiding my tears behind sunglasses, and collapsed on the chair. He'd seen me enter the store and had followed me here, his steps growing more and more agitated when calling my name hadn't slowed my pace.

Dropping at my feet, he placed his hands along the outside of my thighs. "Baby, what's the matter?"

When I didn't respond—because I was too busy choking on misery, so quickly could it return—he slid my sunglasses off my face and kissed the fat drops falling down my cheeks.

This didn't help, but eventually I managed out her name. "*Savannah*."

"What'd she do?" he asked.

I blinked at his self-assumed innocence. "What'd she do to *you*? That's what I want to know." Clutching the wooden arm of the chair so tightly my fingertips went numb, I shoved my chin up in indignation. "What'd you do to *her*?"

"I did nothing," he stated, quite vehemently. "When I got home last night, she was in my bed. And she wouldn't leave, even after I tried to drag her out, so I got Andy and made him deal with her." His eyes probed mine. "I don't know what you heard, but I swear to you, Faryn." His voice wavered with emotion. "I swear I didn't touch her. You are the only one, I promise."

Relief flooded feeling back into my fingertips. "I want to believe you," I told him. "I do, I mean, don't think I don't trust you, or that I'd immediately believe it of you, that you'd do something like that, but Chuck said..." I gulped down what Chuck had said.

"Chuck wants you so bad he can't see straight." He tucked my hair behind my ear. "He was in the kitchen last night. I don't know what he heard, but whatever it was, he misinterpreted."

"He said you looked guilty, getting trashed like you did." Not that he seemed very hung over. Had that been an exaggeration, too?

"If I looked anything, it was disturbed. It wasn't a pleasant experience."

Our eyes locked, and I sighed. "I wish you would've called me, so I could have defended you." I pulled my gaze down to my lap and added weakly, "I wish I could have defended us."

"I'm sorry. I am." He dug around in his pocket and pulled

out a key, offered it to me. "Andy gave this to Savannah. That's how she got in. I want you to have it now. It's my only spare."

I wrapped my hand around it and my arms around his neck.

I wanted to believe him, I did. But I'd only known him for two months. For all I knew, he could be a serial killer. I mean, a person could keep any secret for two months, even a trail of dead bodies.

God knew I had my own secrets that weren't out of the vault yet.

I pulled away with a frown. "I was going to surprise you, take you out to lunch."

Kai rested the back of his hand on my cheek. "You aren't convinced, are you?"

"Of course I am," I lied.

"No. I don't want you to *try* to believe me. It won't work, and it will ruin us. And then she'll win. I will not let her win."

"It's fine," I insisted. But he was right. I was slowly pushing him out of the deepest chamber of my heart. It might happen gradually, the sealing off of the rest of it, but once it began, it was generally difficult to go back.

This might well be the beginning of the end.

"I won't let you do this, Faryn. Come on." He stood and grabbed my hand. I wiped my eyes and attempted to fix my face as he led me through the store and down the street.

"Where are we going?" I asked.

"To talk to Savannah."

I dug my feet in, not sure I could handle such a

confrontation. He squeezed my hand and tugged softly. "I want you to *know*, Faryn. Like I do. If the roles were reversed, I'd be out of my mind. I'd have probably torn your head off." We'd stopped walking, and he faced me, bending a bit to meet my height. "Please come. Please see. Please know?"

And when he looked at me like that, with those dark eyes, well, I might have done anything for him.

We went a few more blocks before he turned into a small office building, led me down a hall, and pushed open a glass door. She was very prickly this morning, Savannah, from where she sat behind the reception desk.

"Hello, Savannah," Kai greeted, cold as ice.

"Hello, Kai," she replied, tart as bitters.

Okay, so that didn't read like two people who'd shared a night together. One small step toward unlocking the truth, one giant leap toward feeling like myself again.

"Faryn heard a rumor this morning-" Kai began.

"Yeah, well, maybe it's not just a rumor," she interrupted.

"And I thought maybe we could all talk about it."

"What do you want to talk about? How hot and steamy it was in your bedroom after?" Her words bit at him in anger, the disappointment of unreciprocated lust clear on her face.

Ah, that felt better.

"Yes, Savannah." I jumped in, now that I'd gotten a hold of things. Paranoia was a terrifying quicksand of desperation, and coming out of it was brilliant. "Please tell me exactly how it happened. I'd like to hear every sordid detail."

She looked over with surprise, and I felt Kai's eyes on me.

I glanced over quickly to assure him I was okay. I knew what I was doing.

"Well," she started, drawing it out like she wanted our attention back on her, "his shirt was off when he came in the room, and I motioned him over to the bed, where I was butt ass naked." She paused for emphasis, but her choice of words only pulled me out of the story. "Then I undid the button on his pants with my teeth, and his zipper with my tongue. I bet you don't know how to do that, do you?"

I crossed my arms. "What about his belt?"

She scoffed. "He doesn't wear belts." But all three sets of our eyes dropped to his waist, where the thick black chastity belt was fastened tightly.

I smirked, satisfied.

"Oh yeah, that belt." She rolled her eyes. "Same thing, no hands. I'm a talented girl."

"You took *that* belt off with your teeth?"

"Yeah. Want me to do it again so you can watch?" She jerked her head toward the hall. "I'll do it all again, in the copy room, if you want to join us."

"No, thank you, I don't really want you near anything that's mine." Turning, I linked my arm through Kai's to pull him out the door.

"Feel better?" he asked as we stepped into the sun.

I tilted my head up to let it soak in. "Much. Thank goodness for that trusty belt of yours."

Catching his arms around me and reeling me to him, he kissed my earlobe, my neck, my jaw, my lips. I grinned into it and wrapped my arms around his back.

"So we're good?" he asked.

"We're perfect."

"Then let's go eat."

14

DINING WITH A MONSTER

Kai

I'd been worried when she insisted on the little café, and I had good reason to be.

My father sat in the corner booth, waving us over with what was surely nefarious intent. Faryn, like a lamb walking oblivious into certain slaughter, waved back and tugged at me to join him.

Cemented, I didn't move, so she let go of me and joined him herself.

That, being even worse, shook me loose.

"This is so perfect, Jim," she said as I approached. "I've wanted us all to get together. Have you ordered yet?"

"No." My dad licked his lips in the face of such easy prey.

"You're just in time." He looked up at me, eyes twinkling. "Sit, Kai."

"I'll sit when I damn well choose to sit," I said.

Faryn gave me a look, but she had no idea who she was dealing with. One could never let their guard down.

My dad chuckled. "All grown up and thinking you run your life, eh? A truly confident man would never be so sensitive."

Faryn turned to him, her shoulder twitching with a soft jerk. "He's certainly confident in bed."

I raised an eyebrow. My father's eyes widened, derailed in his amusement. "Is he now?"

She opened her menu, studying it a moment while we marveled at the words that had just come from her mouth. When she looked up, it was only to ask if the Reuben was any good.

"Not as good as my son, apparently."

Flashing him a smile, she replied, "I wouldn't expect that. Maybe I'll get the chili."

"The chili's hot," I said, sitting down. "Very."

"Oh!" he exclaimed, "how nice of you to join us. On your own time, of course, as if I don't own you."

I moved to stand, but his vise-like grip reached across the table and clamped down on my shoulder. He was that large of a man, that tall, his arms that long, that he held me there, in my seat. Gritting my teeth, I forced myself not to struggle. He loved the struggle. Well, I did too. But not here. Not now. Not in front of Faryn.

"Kindly let go," she said, leaning over the table as if they were sharing a secret. "You wouldn't want your insecurity to show."

He only stared at her, digging huge fingertips further into the base of my shoulder. I couldn't help but fold a little, and grimace, though I didn't want him to see it. Always with the upper hand, because of his size, further hating me that I was built like my mom. And me further hating myself, that I was too slight and too short in comparison, to ever completely win.

"Confidence isn't loud, Jim," Faryn whispered. "If you really want people to believe you have your shit together and control over your son, you wouldn't make such a scene."

With a sneer for her, he dropped his hand like he'd been burnt. "He runs my store because I told him to. And he screws with women the way I taught him."

"Well, I must hand it to you then." Putting her menu down, she folded her arms across the top of it. "The store is immaculate, and he's been quite lovely to me."

He had an odd look on his face, one I'd never seen before. Then he snorted. "Lovely? He sure has you fooled."

"Or maybe he has you fooled," she suggested as the waitress approached. I had to hand it to her. She was keeping him off-balance.

"He'll have the Reuben," Faryn ordered, glancing toward my father. "I'll have the chili." Then she looked at me.

I blinked and turned to Nancy. "The usual," I said. She nodded and left us.

"What's your usual?" Faryn asked me.

"A fuck in the bathroom," my dad supplied.

And without missing a beat, she smirked. "The dirty mouth is from you too, I see."

"Is that supposed to be a compliment?"

She settled back in her seat. "If you're so unhappy with him, why'd you retire so young?"

He frowned at this non-answer. Non-answers had historically gotten me slapped.

"Because I wouldn't work at his store unless he wasn't in it," I explained.

"Because why work when you don't have to?" he snarled.

"So what do you do now?"

"I fish."

"That's it?"

"Yes."

"Do you have a lady friend?"

"No."

"Are you interested in any ladies?"

"No."

"Any men?"

"Excuse me?"

"If you're not interested in any ladies, it would follow that maybe you're interested in a man."

"Absolutely not."

"Must be kind of lonely."

"Screw you, missy, I like my solitude. That's why I fish."

"Well, maybe it's why you're in such a bad mood all the time."

"How do you know what kind of mood I'm in?"

"It shows on your face, the expression you've held most

your life."

He looked at me, my dad, like I might have some sort of advice on how to handle her. Hell if I knew. I'd never seen someone have his number like this.

"I'm very happy," he finally said.

"Happy people don't go around making others miserable," she pointed out.

"Who says I make others miserable?"

"Your son won't work with you."

"My son's a pussy."

"Your son likes pussy. There's a difference."

Now it was my dad's turn to blink. He screwed up his face and crossed his arms, which meant he planned on not speaking for a while. Faryn must have sensed this, because she didn't continue with her questions. Instead, she turned to me. "What's your usual?" she asked again.

"The club sandwich."

She slid her hand up and down my thigh, and for a split second, I wondered who this woman was and how much I didn't know about her.

Scooting a little closer, she began a hushed, teasing sort of conversation with me, effectually swapping my father from the one in control to the one left out.

Frankly, it was fucking masterful.

It took him until our food came before he could no longer stand it. "Where are you from, Faryn?"

"Not here."

"That's not much of an answer."

"Well, it wasn't much of a question." She sipped the chili

off her spoon. "This *is* spicy, but I can't say no one warned me."

"How isn't it much of a question?" he asked.

"Because it tells you nothing about me."

He snorted. "I'd love to hear what you consider a good question."

"I'd be happy to tell you, but then it's yours to answer. A person doesn't answer their own questions."

Biting into his Reuben, he chewed slowly. "I don't like sauerkraut."

"Then you shouldn't have ordered a Reuben," she responded. I would've laughed, if I weren't so dumbstruck.

"I didn't order a Reuben," he grumbled.

"But you said they were apparently not as good as your son, as if that was a surprise to you, that you would have thought them better. So when you were all speechless and holding up the waitress, I figured you'd be happy with it, knowing how very good your son is. See?"

He sunk his thoughts into his sandwich for a moment, then scraped the sauerkraut off and took another bite. "I would've ordered it without the sauerkraut."

"Then don't make me order for you next time."

He opened his mouth, but she spoke first. "What would you do, if you could do anything for one entire day, and who would you choose to do it with?"

Narrowing his eyes, he tried to puzzle her out.

"That's my question," she explained. "And if you won't answer mine, I won't answer yours."

"I'll answer," he said quickly, never the one to back down.

"But I might have to think about it."

"Of course. Think away."

So we chewed and ruminated together, and I decided I'd whisk Faryn off to a deserted island and make babies. Or sand castles. One of the two.

"What would you do?" my father asked after he finished half his sandwich.

"Silly boy, those weren't the rules." She set her spoon down and tilted her head, but in the opposite direction than she normally did. Then again, normally she did it when she was amused or intrigued, not when she was calculating.

He grumbled unintelligibly, but I could tell he was enjoying the game. "I would fish, by myself."

"See, that says so much."

"What's it say?"

"What do you think it says?"

"It says I like to fish alone."

"No, Jim. It says you've given up on people, that they've all disappointed you, and you feel most at home with cold, heartless fish."

"Is that supposed to be an insult?"

"Hey, I'm not the one who said it."

"Yes, you did."

She held up a finger. "I only interpreted what *you* said. I think you're a rather sweet old man, actually. You must be, if you're anything like your son here."

He snorted. "I ain't sweet. And he ain't, either."

"Sweet is sexy, Jim. Maybe you should try it." She leaned over the table again, and this time he leaned, too. I shook my head and let out a muffled laugh of disbelief. Hook, line, and sinker, she had drawn him in. She was running things here. "Maybe you should try it on Nancy," she whispered. "You still have quite an attractive face on you."

"You said it was wrinkly."

She settled back. "I said it shows your most used expression, which doesn't mean it isn't handsome. Only problem is the scowl. And the attitude, of course. Tell her you like her blouse and be nice about it."

"I will not tell her I like her blouse."

"Just try it. See what happens."

"Absolutely not."

Faryn shrugged. "Well, if you're scared."

"I'm not scared," he scoffed.

"Then what's stopping you?"

"Nothing's stopping me."

"So you'll do it."

Faryn finished her chili, and I took bites between watching them. Jim pushed his sandwich away and chewed on his lip while we finished eating, and until Nancy arrived with our bill.

"Is there anything else I can get you?" she asked. Nancy was one of the few who didn't seem intimidated by him. They'd lived next to each other as children, and I'd always wondered if there was some history there, though she still avoided him like the plague, if she could help it.

"Nancy." He cleared his throat, and my eyes jumped to him in surprise. "I must say, that's an awfully pretty blouse you have on there."

"Oh." She furrowed her brow and looked down at it, confused. "Thank you, Jim."

I felt Faryn's leg move next to me, and, judging by the oomph that came out of my father, was pretty sure she kicked him to carry on. He glared at her.

After a silent beat, Faryn smiled at Nancy. "Yes, Jim was just saying it's quite flattering to your figure."

"He was?" Nancy raised a dubious eyebrow.

"He's not the coldhearted old bastard everyone thinks he is," Faryn said. "Really, you just have to crack him open."

Nancy smiled a little, with an old sort of familiarity. "Thank you, Jim. I don't get many compliments around here these days, now that I'm the old lady." She glanced back at her younger cohorts.

"You've hardly aged a day since graduation." Whether he attempted this to be sincere or not, it came out with a smirk.

Faryn kicked him again, but Nancy didn't notice. Instead, she actually blushed.

My fucking girlfriend was creating damn miracles in front of my very eyes. Was she Cupid herself? Was that why I'd gone all gooey in five minutes flat?

My father's leer, in the face of genuine positive reaction, actually softened. I could not fucking believe it, and I almost let out a low whistle. Except that would ruin everything, and I didn't need Faryn's wrath directed my way. No way in hell was I ever going to mess with her, after seeing the monster of all monsters here, putty in her hands.

"I'm not joking," he added, his voice gruff and hands twitching on the table.

"Well, I'm sure you are, but it's nice to hear anyway." Nancy reached down to pat his hand. She patted his fucking hand. "Would you like some dessert? It's on me."

"Oh, I-"

"He'd love some," Faryn decided, pushing at me to get out of the booth. "He'd love some, and he'd love it if you'd join him. We were just leaving." She pulled out a twenty from her wallet and slapped it on the table, then leaned over to whisper in Jim's ear. He grumbled, she said something else, and then we were moving.

"What'd you say to him?" I asked, halfway down the block when I was able to speak.

"I told him to be nice."

"And he said?"

"He didn't like the idea."

I laughed. "No shit. And then what'd you say?"

"I told him if he wanted to get laid, he better listen to me." She shrugged. "I think he just might."

Taking off at a jog, she ran the few blocks back to the store and waited for me by the soda machine. There, she grabbed my hand and led me to my office.

"Well, that was nice," she said, her back against the closed door.

"Was it?" I asked.

"You didn't think so?"

"I think..." I sat down at my desk chair, still somewhat stunned. "I think that was insane. You were incredible with him. I mean, you're always incredible, but-"

"You're sure?"

"I'm sure what?"

"You're sure I'm always incredible?" She pushed herself off the door and came to sit in my lap. "Or did I only reach incredibility back there, just now?"

"Of course you're always incredible. It was just a different kind of incredible. I wasn't expecting you to handle him. You handled him. You actually *handled* my father. No one has ever handled my father." I let out a big laugh.

"He reminds me of someone," she said, gaze averted toward the cheap photo art hanging on my wall, voice trailing off like I'd lost her to it.

"Who?"

"It's not important. Anyway, what's with Andy? How come he didn't come over and say hi?" Andy had been at the counter, eating a quiet lunch and glancing at us every so often.

"Andy and my dad don't get along."

"Why not?"

"If you hadn't noticed, Jim's a monster."

She frowned.

"What?" I poked her with a fingertip when she didn't respond. "Really, tell me something. Let me crack you open a little." I used finger quotes on the phrase she'd used on Nancy.

"It's nothing, I was just thinking."

"Thinking what?"

She closed her eyes. "That if you've looked into the face of a demon, a monster doesn't seem so bad."

I let the severity of that settle in. Then, "This demon is

who he reminds you of?"

Her eyes opened, and she shook her head. "I'm sorry, I shouldn't have said anything."

"Why not?"

"Because I don't want to talk about it." She kissed me on the nose and stood. "You probably have a lot of work to do anyway. I'll see you later?"

"Stay."

She grinned, seeming to shed all of what had just happened. "Don't worry, I'll be impatiently waiting for more of you."

I reached for her hand and squeezed it. "I'll bring me as quickly as I can."

15

THE LAST STAND

Andy

Who the fuck she think she was, comin' in here and ruin_n' my life? I'd hardly been able to believe it, watchin' her sit there with Kai and his dad. No one sat with Kai and his dad. What'd that mean anyway? Did it mean they were engaged already? Did it mean there was no turnin' back?

There better be turnin' back, and I'd been lazy to let it get this far. Sittin' on the side, waitin' it out, sure Kai wouldn't sacrifice himself for some stupid broad. But wouldn't you know it. One look at Faryn and he turned the damn world upside down.

Well, enough o' that. It's not like it was just his world she was messing with. It was mine, too. And I was sick of it.

I pounded loud on her door, the shots I'd downed moments ago helping to both spur me on and cool me down. Knock, knock, knock, and again. Knock, knock, knock, and she answered, looking all surprised and shit, like I wasn't good enough to pay her a visit.

Bitch.

"Andy?"

"Hey there, baby cakes." I grinned lewdly, but it couldn't be helped. When I was drinkin', the smiles just came out that way.

She frowned and perched a hip against the frame, pulling the door close to her. "Are you looking for Kai?"

"Nah, I already tried talking to him." Besides, I knew he wasn't here, 'cuz I'd watched him leave. "I thought maybe we could talk," I said. "Thought maybe you'd understand me better than he did."

"Talk about what, Andy?"

"I miss my friend, Faryn. And chicks, well, y'all talk all the time. I tried to talk to Kai, but he don't get it."

She glanced down at my feet, one of which was inching toward her. I had to make her understand, but her eyes were all wide and shit, like I scared her, so I pulled my shoe back. Sweet talk, that's what she'd fall for. I sugared up my voice best I could.

"I jus' need a shoulder to cry on." Really I was gonna tell her why they were all wrong for each other, but I knew I had to play my cards right. Faryn was a shifty one. Kai might not get that, but it's all I saw, and I had to be careful.

Though that leg she was showin' under those little peejay

shorts was not helpin' me stay focused.

"You don't strike me as the crying type, Andy."

And that was a damn tight tank top. "Listen, maybe we can talk out some sort of deal, you know? So we can both have him."

"I think you need to take that up with Kai."

"Kai won't listen to me," I grumbled. "He can't hear shit right now."

"I'm sorry, Andy." She set her head on the doorframe. "I'll try to be more sensitive to the two of you spending time together."

Did that mean she wasn't sensitive now? Is that why he was never around? She probably was, all controlling and shifty. Bitch.

But I couldn't get angry, not yet. So I gave her my puppy dog eyes, the only thing I'd been natural blessed with. "Won't cha let me in so we can talk about it?"

"What is it you think talking will solve?"

This wasn't workin'. If I were gonna convince her that Kai was shit, she had to wanna pay attention to me.

I squinted my eyes a bit, so they might look like I was cryin'. "I jus' need someone to talk to, Faryn." I smacked my hand to my heart. "I'm hurtin', you know? And I ain't used to that."

"Kai's free right now, Andy. Maybe you guys could hang out. Want me to call him?"

"He'd be so mad at me comin' here, you know, with his temper and all." I screwed up my face. Emotion, fake emotion and puppy dog eyes, that's all I had. Well, and a killer body. With a face like mine, I needed to work the other angles best I could. "He don't want nobody messin' with you, and I get that. You're special to him. But I don't know where to go. Buddy at work, maybe, but he'd just laugh at me. We guys, we don't share stuff like this. And Kai, I'm sorry but he ain't thinkin' of nothin' but you right now. The way he talks, well, I just figgered you'd know what to do. I'm lookin' for someone to tell me what to do, tell me how to get my friend back."

Everything was quiet, but I could feel her turnin', so I held still. Finally, she sighed and put up a finger, left the door open a crack, and disappeared.

Damn, I coulda been a movie star.

Returning with a sweater, she slipped into the hall. "Let's go sit on the steps."

We sat all the long way at the bottom, and first thing I did was put my head in my hands to try out a few sobs. "Please don't tell Kai I was here, 'kay?" I sniffled. "He'd seriously beat my ass."

"Oh, he would not," she soothed. "You're his best friend."

"He knocked my teeth out when we were nineteen for sleepin' with his girlfriend." I looked over to her. "But he slept with mine first. It was only fair."

I fought to keep in my smile, 'cuz she was finally swingin' my way, I could tell. Her face was all thinkin' and confused.

"Then he broke my nose when we were twenty-two, o'er nothin'. Ain't you seen his temper yet? Most people see that before they meet his dad. Heck, just about nobody meets his dad. And not 'cuz no one can stand Jim, but 'cuz Kai don't want no one seein' that the apple is sitting right on the damn trunk o' the tree." I waited for a response, and wondered if maybe she didn't get it, what I was tryin' to say. "That means Kai and Jim, they the same person."

She'd been lookin' out at the street, and here she turned to me. "Kai is nothing like his father. And if you don't know that, then you aren't as good a friend as you say you are."

"You believe that, it's cuz you ain't seen his bad side. He'll start drinkin', havin' sex, beatin' people up, lyin', cheatin'. There ain't much he hasn't done, and there ain't much he wouldn't do, in one o' those moods a his." I tsked. "Like that other night. He all pissed at Savannah and about to run a rage, I'm the one who had to hold him back. I'm always the one who has to hold him back, the only one who's ever been able to do it. And I guarantee you me, you'll want me there when the time comes." This was sort of true. Most often I got juiced up when Kai got in a fight, but there'd been a few times I'd been the calmer head. "He goes crazy nuts, like a rabies bear on steroids. You sure don't wanna see that." I shook my head like I knew what I was talkin' about.

"Andy, why are you here?"

I started crying again. It gave me some time to find a new angle. "Everyone's growin' up around me. I don't get it. Why can't I find anyone to grow up with? Why doesn't anyone love me like that?"

She curled her hands into her chest. Like she wanted me to look there. "I don't know, Andy. I don't really know you."

"And you don't even want to know me, do you?" I was a little bitter about this. She hadn't given me the time of day after that Bloody Mary. Lewis was good enough to spend hours with, but not me? I was Kai's best damn friend. She should've taken some time with me.

"That's not fair, Andy," she responded. "I don't have a lot of friends, I know, but that's not about you. It's just how I work."

"And how *do* you work?" I turned my head so she wouldn't see me gettin' all pissed.

"I don't get close to too many people, Andy. I can't." Her voice broke, and I wondered if I was finally gettin' somewhere.

"So I'm not good enough then?" I let my voice break too, and she set a hand on my shoulder. Almost like a real hug.

"Of course you're good enough. I just don't have time for two…people." She choked on the last word, and the smell of her so damn close filled my nose.

Her sweater slipped off her shoulder and as she slid it back up, her chest slid along my arm.

Like she meant it to. Planting my hand on her breast, I smashed my lips to hers. A shudder shook her, and I could hardly believe my luck.

But then a scream, inside my mouth. Well, fuck her and what she'd done to me. She could at least give me what I wanted for once. I held on tighter and kissed her harder. She clawed at my hand, tryin' to pull it off her chest, but I had her head and wouldn't let go.

I got it now, what Kai liked, and was really gettin' into it, when somebody grabbed my shoulder and yanked me off balance.

I had to let go of her in order to catch myself, but I fell off the steps anyway. The gravel path cut up my palm, and fuckin' Leon stood there, ruinin' my night.

Faryn was horrified, the bitch, hands all clasped over her mouth. What the hell was so horrifying about me? She scrambled to her feet and shot up the stairs without one look back.

Fuck.

"Get outta here before I call Kai," Leon threatened. And with that, I scrambled as fast as Faryn had.

I peeled out of the parking lot, turned the corner, and braked to the curb.

That had not gone as planned. I slammed my hands on the wheel and winced in pain. There was shit all caught up in my skin, and it hurt like I needed a damn nurse.

Now what?

Now Faryn wouldn't get near me, and if Kai ever found out, he'd kill me. Would she tell him? Did I need to go back up there and scare her so she wouldn't?

But there was no way Leon wasn't keeping an eye out.

I ground my torn-up palms into my steering wheel until I decided I couldn't leave it like that. I had to try and apologize, or threaten her, or something. Kai could never find out.

So I swung the car door open and hid in the darkness behind the gas station, quick climbed the retaining wall that separated the properties, and snuck up her stairs. After tiptoeing down the hall, so no one would hear me, I knocked soft.

She didn't answer, and I didn't hear a thing.

I knocked again, a little harder this time, then seethed her name through my teeth as loud as I dared.

Nothing.

I started pounding, harder and harder, not caring anymore if Leon came for me. I'd kick him right back down those steps. This bitch better not ruin everything. If she told Kai, she'd fucking ruin everything she hadn't already ruined. What if she was on the phone with him right now? It was making me fucking crazy, the thought of it.

Finally, the door opened a crack, and a crazy eye looked out. I curled my hand around the wood to make sure she wouldn't close it, but she slammed the door shut on my fingers. "Fuck! You bitch!" I screamed.

"Leave me the hell alone," she said, quiet and mean.

Kai always went on about how soft she was, but this shit wasn't soft. My knuckles had been scraped clean, for fuck's sake. "Don't fuckin' tell him I was here," I warned.

She pulled the door back open a crack. "Don't fucking touch me again."

"Don't tell him I was here!" I shouted, almost fucking frantic. Who the hell did she think she was? "I will kill you if you ruin my life any more than you already have, you hear me? I'll *kill* you!"

I'd never been one to follow through with threats, not like Kai, but she had fucking slammed my finger in the damn door. I sure as shit would kill her, she so much as looked at me again.

"You don't want to mess with me, Andy. You have no idea what I'm capable of."

"Pretty tough with a door between us, aren't you?" I spat in her face but she slammed the door again.

I pounded both fists on the old wood, imagining I could fucking split it in half, then left before anyone found me. Sure enough, Leon was comin' round the corner as I came out the stairs and slipped around the house. Like her own private guard.

Back in my truck, I spun the wheels off the curb and headed to Savannah's. Savannah would understand. We were in this together. She wanted Kai back as bad as I did.

I revved the engine in her driveway to burn off some steam, and by the time I made it to the front door, she was waitin' for me. With one look at my hand, she let me in. Savannah lived in a little duplex and had dressed it up real nice.

I made to stand in the entry, but she pushed me toward the bathroom and pulled out a first-aid kit.

"What the hell happened to you?" she asked.

"Damn, you look hot," I said. She had on a slinky, see-through nightie, and I could just make out the goods. She smiled at me, and I realized I'd woke her up, hair all over the place, eyes all sleepy-like. "I didn't mean to wake you."

Taking my hand, she ran it under cool water, which helped.

"What happened?" she repeated.

"I slammed my finger in the car door."

"So why'd you come here, of all places?"

Oh yeah. That. I shifted my weight from one foot to the other. "Are you attracted to me, Savannah?"

"What?"

"Are you attracted to me? I mean, I know my face is scarred as fuck, but I ain't the ugliest guy you ever seen, right? Have you seen my abs?"

Studying me for only a beat before going back to my hand, she said, "Sure, I could be attracted to you."

"I have a plan," I said. She pushed her lips out in response, and I enjoyed that a second before explaining. "I'm gonna get you pregnant so Kai has to take you back."

She wrinkled her nose. "Why would he take me back if I were pregnant with your baby?"

"Because we'd make him think it was his."

She thought about this while I stared at her chest. Then she thought about it some more while I tried to figure what I could see through her lace panties. It was pretty dark though, the only light from the hallway behind me. I moved over so it would shine on her.

Aw, yeah. There we go.

Squinting, she reached around me to flip off the light switch in the hall.

Damn. Too bad.

"Kai and I haven't had sex in a month and a half," she said.

"Then we'd better get started."

She looked at me all serious for a minute, then nodded and grinned. Then—get the fuck this—she lifted her top off.

"You are some seriously hot stuff," I said. In my experience, it was always better if you pumped them up on the way in. Maybe had I done that with Faryn, it wouldn't a gone so bad.

We ripped our clothes off and went to town right there in the bathroom. It was the hottest sex I'd ever had, and I told her that too, when we were done. We sat side by side on the cold tile floor and I flicked my cigarette ash into her toilet. She tapped her feet together, legs all stretched out, nice and long.

"You ain't so bad yourself," she said. "Kai's got nothing on you."

I let the grin take over my face. At least someone thought so.

"What if it doesn't work?" she asked. "What if I'm not pregnant?"

I turned to her. "Wanna try again, to make sure?"

She thought about it a moment, then straddled me and jammed her hips into mine. "We might have to keep trying," she said, "over and over until we know."

"Fine by me, baby cakes," I said, flicking my cigarette butt in the toilet and holding on for the ride. "That is fucking fine by me."

16

PAST AND PRESENT

Faryn

I woke up the next morning, feeling off.

Andy had thrown me the night before, not to mention my head was pounding. This, apparently, from the entire bottle of wine I'd finished after the whole debacle. Groaning as I made my way to the bathroom, I paused in the doorway to take in the small, blue-tiled space.

I did not remember making a mess in here last night. Obviously, I'd been drunk off my rocker. Sliding the drawers shut, I restacked the pill bottles in the medicine cabinet and swung the mirror back in place.

Whatever painkillers I'd taken as a preemptive measure before bed definitely hadn't paid off. I hardly looked like I'd slept at all, and I sent up a quick prayer that my insomnia wasn't coming back.

In my experience, insomnia led to nightmares. Nightmares so bad they were more accurately described as night terrors, but I wasn't going to think about that.

After turning on the shower, I came back to my reflection. My wheat blond hair naturally held the loosest of curves, and my face was round in every way: big eyes, small nose, plump lips. My eyes were brown, framed thickly with lashes, and my cheeks soft.

It sounded good on paper, but right now I looked like crap. I looked like crap, and I felt like crap. It had been a rough night.

Stripping down, I stepped in the shower, hoping to rinse some of it off, but by the time I had my coffee and made it to work, I didn't feel any better.

I guess that's what a bottle of wine will do to you.

"Morning, sunshine," Lewis greeted as I walked in and removed my sunglasses. Sometimes it paid to work at a bar, where the light wasn't so offensive.

"Hey, Lewis."

Chuck studied me, then walked over and tilted my chin up with his hand. "Wow, is our Miss Faryn actually hung over?"

I gave him a look. "I never said I didn't drink."

"No, but you never have."

"Why would you want me drinking at work?"

He shrugged. "Sometimes hot bartenders drink at work and then dance on the bar. It brings in crowds. Though, screw the crowds, I'd be happy you just dancin' for me."

"Yeah, yeah," I said. "Not today, okay?"

"Rough night, kid?" Lewis asked.

"I guess." Rounding the bar, I sat next to him. My current plan was not to stand any more than I had to.

"I take it I was right then?" Chuck asked. "Kai did the dirty with Savannah?"

"Oh, no actually." I'd forgotten all about that. "I talked to her, and it was obvious she tried to seduce him, but it didn't work."

Chuck's face darkened. "So what'd he do to you?"

"Nothing." I pressed my fingertips to my raging temples and sat down next to Lewis, laying my head in my arms. "What do you mean, what'd he do to me?"

"You said you had a rough night. Why'd you have a rough night?"

"Lay off, Charles," Lewis said softly. "She'll talk if she wants to."

"It's okay, there's not much to talk about. Just some personal stuff." I hadn't decided if I was going to tell Kai about Andy, but no matter how I looked at it, it didn't make much sense. I'd already been a strain on their relationship and whatever I thought of Andy, it didn't change the fact he was, and always had been, Kai's best friend.

I didn't want to cause more trouble, and what if it didn't work out with us in the long run? As much as I felt like Kai was where I was supposed to land, that didn't mean we were bulletproof. Not yet. If things didn't work out, and Kai didn't have his best friend to fall back to, well, I wouldn't feel right about that.

"He's no good, Faryn," Chuck said. I peeked out at him from my cradled arms as he started drying the tray of glasses sitting on the bar. Usually I did this, but I guess I looked bad enough he was going to let me be.

"He used to get in fights all the time," Chuck said, after I looked away from him. "Bad ones, the kind that ended with him in lockup. Once, he was even charged with battery."

I readjusted my limp head, so I could see Lewis. "Are we talking about Andy?"

Lewis shook his head. "Kai's always been the bad boy. Andy just enjoyed the ride."

"Maybe it was twice," Chuck amended. "You really want a boyfriend that's got a record? Battery, theft, I think he even burned his dad's garage down when he was a kid—on purpose."

"Chuck." I sighed. "Are you telling me you don't have a past you're ashamed of?"

"No, I don't, Faryn. I may not look like much, but I've never been one to get in trouble." He put a glass away with a heavier than average thud and turned back to challenge me. "Are you trying to tell me you know all this? That he's told you all the horrible things he's done? He tell you about the time he stole a car?"

I didn't answer.

"Yeah, I didn't think so. He puts on such a damn show for you, of course he wouldn't want to ruin the image. But it's all fake. He used to hang me by my ankles from the fucking tree in front of my house." Chuck slammed another glass down, so hard this time I jumped up straight. "That the kind of guy you want?" he challenged. "He *tortured* me."

I could see it suddenly, the short, skinny kid he'd been. "I'm sorry, Chuck."

"Well, somebody should be." But his vigor faded.

"May I ask why you're telling me this now?"

We stared at each other, and Lewis finally answered for him. "They'd made peace, maybe five years ago, so he didn't hate him when you showed up. Now he hates him again."

"I don't get what you could possibly see in him." Chuck shook his head. "You seem so much smarter than a girl who falls for a pretty face."

"He's not just a pretty face."

"Hey, fancy that. I'm not either." He stood nervously in front of me, after this plug for himself.

"Chuck, I won't date my boss."

"Then you're fired." He cracked a small but sad smile at this. "Problem solved."

I clutched my forehead with two fingertips, pressing them in to relieve the pressure. This day was not getting better. "Chuck, I'm not leaving Kai. Fire me if you want, but it won't change anything."

"I'm not going to fire you, Faryn." His eyes danced quickly over mine, and he went back to his drying. "That's the last thing I would do."

The door opened, and I covered my eyes as the harsh light intruded.

"Speak o' the devil," Lewis whispered.

Before I had time to drink in the face that might actually help me feel better, his hands were on my shoulders.

Spinning on the stool, I grabbed him around the waist and squeezed as tightly as I could. He ran his fingers through my hair, and I let myself fall into him.

"Well, well, well," said a rough, sandpaper voice.

My eyes popped open to find Jim standing behind him. I let go and stood up. "Hi, Mr. Allen."

"You work here or somethin'? You don't look like much for grunt work."

"Leave her alone," Kai warned, his expression meeting and raising that of his father's.

"I thought we were friends, Jim." I didn't have the energy to deal with him today, I just didn't. Not even the most vicious, irritable, protective piece of me was up for it, after the night we'd had.

"Why would we be friends after you forced that horrible, babbling woman on me?"

"Didn't go so well?"

"How 'bout you make it up to me by getting us a table. And quick like a rabbit."

Kai sent me an apologetic look while I directed them to the nearest one, even though Chuck's patrons generally sat themselves. Jim had to know this.

"I'll give you a minute to decide what you want," I said.

"I don't want to sit here any longer than I have to," Jim replied. "Just take our order now."

"Of course."

"I thought you wanted to have lunch with me." Kai spit this quietly across the table. "You asked to have lunch with me." Furtively, he glanced at Chuck and Lewis, as if they hadn't already lived a lifetime in the same town, as if they might not already know about the legendary dysfunction inside the Allen household. "You practically begged me."

"And we're having lunch. You got a problem with that?" Jim's steely eyes narrowed into black points, and there was a dare implicit in these words, as if the usual answer had started many a fight before.

"Excuse me," I interrupted. "But would you like me to come back for your order?"

Kai slumped in his seat and reached for my hand. I squeezed it, for both our sakes.

"This is a business meeting, Kai. About how you're ruining my store."

"I'm not ruining shit," Kai grumbled.

"I'll come back," I said.

"No, you won't." Kai's father stared at me, daring me to suggest anything different. I wasn't sure I'd ever met anyone so fond of intimidation. It fatigued me. "We'll both have burgers," he said. "And now you may go."

He'd baited and reeled me in, all so he could tear his son down in front of an audience? "Wow. You *are* an asshole." But he didn't hear me. I released it as I swung back behind the bar and took the towel from Chuck. "You hear that?" I asked.

"That Kai's dad's an asshole? I've known that my whole life."

"No, the order."

"Yes, I heard it." He smiled a little at me, and this was the Chuck I liked, the one who didn't try too hard. He and I, we got along, and we got along well. "Two cheeseburgers, coming right up."

Setting the towel down, I got them water, finished drying the glasses, wiped down the bar, and straightened the shelves. There wasn't much else. I'd vacuum, but that was rude unless it was just the three of us, and it would probably hurt like taking an axe to my head. So I settled next to and across from Lewis, hands flat on the long stretch of wood, to watch Kai and his dad together.

They weren't talking, but Kai seemed to shrink with every passing moment.

Chuck came toward me with their plates, but when I went to take them he shrugged me off. Walking over with his skinny gait, he slammed the dishes down on the table and turned to march back to the kitchen.

"What the hell was that?" Kai's dad asked.

"Maybe he doesn't appreciate your business," Kai muttered.

"Maybe he doesn't appreciate you fucking his waitress," his dad countered.

"Too bad I'm not fucking his waitress, or I might have to beat the shit out of you right here."

"You're not? What the hell's the point then?"

"I thought this was supposed to be a business meeting."

"This is a business meeting."

"Yeah, these business meetings are always so productive."

Jim slammed his hand on the table. The silverware jumped. "That's still my damn store, you hear? I own it. And until I die, I own everything in it. That includes you."

Lewis raised a brow in my direction, and I watched,

curious.

"What the hell you lookin' at?" Jim yelled across the room. "You ain't got nothin' better to do?"

I shook my head. "I really don't," I said. "Plus, you are talking about me."

"This is what he's gonna be some day," he cried, tapping at his own chest.

"Sadly, you aren't the first to bring that up," I muttered. Kai closed his eyes with this, defeated?

"He's down on me now," Jim continued, "but mark my words, I'm what he'll grow into. That what you want? You ready for this?"

Looking at Kai and not his father, I responded softly, "I think I might be."

No one heard me but Lewis. He smiled.

Kai shoved half his burger in his mouth at once, and they carried on in their angry way. When they'd finished, having accomplished absolutely nothing—Kai offered a few minor reports on how the store was doing, Jim said it did better when he ran it, Kai called bullshit, that sort of thing—I cleared the table, set the dishes on the bar for Chuck, and pretended I was going to the bathroom. The little square hall was dark, and I hoped Kai would meet me, to steal a moment, before he went back to work.

He did.

I reached out for him, and he wrapped his arms around me, hiding his face in my neck.

"I missed you," I said. "I had a rough night."

He straightened. "What happened?"

"Oh, nothing in particular." He was having a bad enough day as it was. "You'll come back after work?"

"Of course. I'd stay now, if I could."

I tilted my head with a smile. "Stay now."

"You make everything better," he professed. "I'd *never* leave you, if I could help it."

"And you," I replied, "make sense of me."

His resulting kiss was fervent in the rawness his troubled relationship with his father had brought to the surface. I went back at him the same, trying to regain some of the control I'd recently lost. It gave me a point of reference, something to focus on when I was scattered.

When I came out of his embrace, my head hurt less. Finally.

"Come back immediately," I told him. "As soon as you can."

"And you'll tell me about last night?"

"There's not much to tell, really, just old demons." Well, old and new, I guess.

"I can understand old demons."

I blinked at him, wondering if he was talking about his father or the things he'd done. "Chuck told me you stole a car, among other things. He told me about your demons."

His eyes narrowed. "That Chuck has a loose mouth."

I smirked. "He'd probably be very happy someone thinks so."

"It doesn't bother you?" he asked.

"Kai!" his dad yelled. "Get your fuck over and let's get on with our day!"

"I'm so sorry."

Shaking my head, I rested a palm on his cheek. "You are not your dad, Kai. I can promise you that."

"Does that mean it doesn't bother you, what Chuck said?"

"Of course it doesn't bother me, unless you're still doing it." Kissing him quickly, I curled my fingertips over his belt. "I don't care that no one knows about this belt, Kai. I know about it, and that's what matters. I know you've changed, that you *are* changing, that you didn't sleep with Savannah when maybe the old Kai would have. I don't care what they think. I care what I know."

He stared at me, dark eyes full of emotion, and we were caught in the first understanding that we knew each other better than anyone else might know us, the people we were right now. We'd fallen in that far, landing in a place that was ours and ours alone. No one could touch us here.

Kai broke the trance. "I don't think I was a jerk because I was his son. I think I was a jerk because he made damn sure I was."

"It doesn't matter what you were, Kai. It matters what you are now." This was the nugget I'd held onto since moving here. I was trying to be what I wanted to be. I was trying to be whole.

"Now you know all my secrets, and I know none of yours."

I chewed on my lip, not sure I was ready. There were so many, and all interconnected like a thick ball of double-sided tape. I didn't know what would happen if I tried to ease into it by sharing only one, but feared they'd all come cascading out, unstoppable, undeniable, and ugly as hell.

He frowned. "Forget I said anything. It's not important."

"I had a fiancé," I blurted out.

"Had?"

"Yes. I left him. And now I know why I did."

He wrapped himself as tightly around me as he was able. I ached to cry, on the brink of some emotional charge I didn't quite have control over.

It had been a rough night.

"Kai!" Jim was nearer now, so Kai wasted no time releasing me. It was painful, but I understood. Jim and his evil, intruding on this little space of ours, would be devastating.

Approaching his father, Kai pulled out his wallet and placed a twenty on the table. Moving to the door at the same pace, without any further goodbyes, they left, and I felt myself unraveling as he went.

17

COMPLETION

Faryn

That entire week, I had trouble sleeping. And the next, until about all I could do during the day was drag my feet from place to place. Insomnia took a toll on me, but the night terrors were even worse. I would rather not sleep than be trapped inside one of those. Needless to say, I drank copious amounts of coffee, and Chuck even went so far as to send me home early—on a Saturday. He'd taken one look at me after my lunch hour, during which I'd fallen asleep for approximately thirteen minutes, and shoved me out the door for more.

If only he knew it wouldn't be so easy.

I changed, called Kai at work to tell him I wouldn't be at

the bar later, then sat on my couch in a daze.

I couldn't figure the stressor. There'd always been a stressor.

I was used to a pretty intense life, had been at one hard for the last fifteen years. In the face of that, how could this simple day-to-day affect me? Unless I'd gotten so used to the simplicity here, my threshold was now that much lower.

With tears of failure and defeat, I pulled out my journal from beneath the couch cushion and paged through the tattered pages. You could easily spot the hardest times in my life from the more hurried, tortured script. It had been enough, at those points, to have a coherent thought.

Paging through until I found the last one, I read what I'd put to paper, documenting my decision to run:

It often takes more courage to stop a pursuit than it does to start. Starting requires initiative and guts and a thirst for glory, but ending requires humility and surrender. Surrender that the glory is over, or that one's quest for it was never satisfied in the first place. The thirst for success is enough to drive most any of us, but the humility and surrender is a much greater feat, for it is so very much harder to find.

It hadn't been easy, deciding to leave everyone and everything behind. But I'd found enough strength in this rumination to at least get me packed up and out the door before having to make any explanations. And ultimately, I did it for them. I was no good unless I was whole and centered, and I'd dropped so many pieces, causing more problems than I was worth. I hadn't wanted to burden them with that and had seen this as my last chance, my final stand.

But now I seemed headed in the wrong direction, back into an abyss more terrifying than anything this world could throw at me.

Kai had a key now, and I heard him as he turned the lock. Calling cheerfully, he found me as I stuffed my journal back in its hiding space, the tears dripping past my nose.

Sitting down, he scooted close and wrapped his arms around me. I rested my head on his chest and let it out, all of it, as he ran a hand through my hair and made soft hushing noises. They were gentle and meant to soothe, not anxious or impatient, which just made me cry harder.

Until it was all out and I was spent.

He wiped the remains of my tears from my cheeks and kissed my eyes, first one and then the other.

I grabbed a few more tissues.

"I'm sorry," I whispered.

He shook his head. "Don't be."

"I can't sleep, Kai."

"I know."

"I'm so exhausted, fighting it."

"What do you mean?" he asked. "You're *trying* not to sleep?"

I closed my eyes. "When I do, I have nightmares. But I don't wake up from them knowing they aren't real. I mean, I *know* they aren't real, but they *feel* real, and I can't shake the feeling they leave me with."

"What feeling?"

I shuddered. "Like someone is watching me."

"Like, in your apartment? You think someone has been in your apartment, and you haven't mentioned it?"

"It's probably just the ghost stories," I muttered. "Anyway, with the few hours of sleep I'm getting, my mind could easily be playing tricks on me."

"What do you mean, tricks? What are you talking about?" The muscles in his arms tightened, and I ran my fingers along them.

"Well, my books have been rearranged." I motioned to the small section of built-in shelves inside the arch that led to the kitchen. "They used to be by genre, but now they're alphabetized, starting with the L's."

He unwound himself and knelt in front of them. "Is there some sort of message in that? *L* for love or something?"

"Kai, I'm sure it was just me. Sometimes, when I can't sleep, I do stuff like that."

"Do stuff like *what?*" he asked, incredulous.

"Reorganize, you know? Busy work." I ran my hands over my face, now defensive. "When was the last time *you* spent hours staring at the ceiling, wishing you could sleep, but knowing you couldn't? You really have no idea how violently frustrating it can be."

"Faryn. You have no deadbolt on your door, that rusty chain you never use could bust of its own accord, and when you *do* sleep you don't hear my calls, even with your cell phone ringing that obnoxious noise a foot from your ear. Do you have any idea how easy it would be for someone to be snooping around in here?"

I sighed. I had to give him that. Real sleep was blissful and all-encompassing.

A look of horror crossed his face. "My God, to think what they could have been doing besides snooping." He pulled the books out one by one to riffle their pages, dropping them to the floor only once he was certain there was nothing stuffed inside.

When he finished, he asked, "Is this it? Is there anything else?"

I didn't want to tell him because I was sounding crazy. Who doesn't remember chunks of midnight time, and what they did in their half-dazed state?

An insomniac, that's who, but unless you're an insomniac, you can't really understand.

"Faryn, please, there are enough creepy people in this town. If you don't let me help you figure it out, I'm calling the cops right now."

"Okay, okay." I put my hand up. "But like I said, it could have been me."

He frowned. "It was *not* you. And I can't believe you didn't tell me earlier. I would have never let you sleep here alone."

It was one of his precautions, not spending the night until our ninety days were up. I didn't want him to sacrifice that. "Kai-"

"No. I'm not leaving. I will stay here tonight, and the next night, and the next, and whatever son of a bitch tries to cross that threshold will find themselves flying right out the fucking window."

I watched him for a moment, morphed into a determined

protector. It took only that for me to submit, to surrender. Better him than me. I was too tired to protect myself right now. "All my candles and decorations, I group them in threes normally. Odd numbers always look better."

He surveyed the room, and I followed his gaze. Everything was in pairs. He quickly began to readjust, and the longer he spent on it, the more agitated he got. He went through the entire apartment before coming back to stand in front of me.

"Maybe I'm the third," I suggested with a weak smile, "and the ghosts want me out."

"There are no damn ghosts, for fuck's sake. How do you not think this is a stalker?" He was almost shouting at me. "I'm the third, the one the SOB wants to get rid of." He ran his hand through his short hair, stopping to clench the crown of his head. "Who could L stand for? Lewis, Leon? What about Chuck? He refers to himself every chance he gets as Lover Boy, what if it's him?"

I blinked. It did make sense. I hadn't put those pieces together in the same way, but it did make sense.

The thought of someone actually in my apartment broke me out in goose bumps.

"What was your fiancé's name?" he asked.

I shook my head; it wasn't him. He was as levelheaded and sane as they came.

"What is it?" he asked again.

"He doesn't know where I am. No one does."

"What is it?" he demanded.

"Spencer," I whispered. "Spencer Larson."

He nodded and turned, dropping down next to me. "This

is fucking impossible."

"It's not him. I promise."

"It could be anyone."

I grasped for his hand, and he clung to it with both of his.

"Screw my rules, Faryn. I'm spending the night. I'm spending every night."

Relieved at his tenacity and reassured by the thought of his constant presence, the stress that had been stuck behind my eyes for weeks dissipated, leaving me in a pleasant sort of space.

"Are you hungry?" I asked. I was hungry. When had I eaten last?

He studied me. "I guess."

I looked out the window, at the warm end-of-summer rain that had picked up, and decided I wanted to stay right here. "Wanna order pizza?"

"Sure."

But by the time the pizza came, I'd fallen asleep. We'd been talking, me all wrapped up in him, and I dozed off. I could vaguely recall the knock at the door and him getting up to retrieve our dinner, but I didn't actually wake.

Kai's presence must have been all the security I needed, because when I was finally able to rouse myself, we were in bed, my cheek rested on his lap, arm curled around the bare skin of his side.

An afternoon kind of light shimmered through the window, and I shot up, alarmed. "What time is it?"

He chuckled, and I turned. He was on top of the covers, propped up on a multitude of pillows with my book in his hand and his shirt off. Wow, had I been under.

"Seriously, what day is it?"

"It's just tomorrow." He nodded toward the clock. "About four pm."

"I missed work?"

"I called you in sick. Chuck didn't seem all that surprised."

"*You* missed work?" I was mortified at this. And that someone else, besides myself, had called me in.

"They can function without me." He set my book down. I'd gotten it at the grocery store, since they didn't have much in the way of an actual bookstore in town. It was totally slutty, and I made a face at it.

"Yeah, high quality reads you got here." He made a face too, one I couldn't decipher. "*Totally* put me in the mood."

With a grin, I crawled up next to him and ran my hand up and down his chest. Oh, his chest.

"I slept for almost twenty-four hours? Without nightmares or terrors?" Dropping my lips down on the cusp of his shoulder, I added, "I feel better than I have in weeks. I don't know how I could possibly thank you."

He raised an eyebrow. "I think you did, letting me read that book."

"And you'll do this again tonight?"

"Every night, Faryn."

"But did you sleep?"

"After I rigged up a booby trap by the door, yes."

"Really?"

"Really."

I hopped up to check it out. It was a rather ingenious

contraption, silverware attached to strings and plastic tumblers piled high on the edge of a chair. The chair alone, shoved up under the doorknob, probably would have been enough.

I couldn't pass the bathroom without brushing my teeth, and the shower was right there too. I needed a shower.

Returning to the bedroom in a towel, I squeezed into my closet to change. Some days I couldn't help tease him, but others I didn't want to make it any harder than it already was.

Once dressed, I made my way back to the bed.

He put my book down again, and I noticed with a start that his belt was off. Cocking my head, I curled my fingers around the waistband of his jeans.

"I figured it had to be hella uncomfortable on your face," he said. "And it's been ninety days since I first walked into that bar."

"It has?"

He nodded. "Yesterday."

"Yesterday?" I gasped. "And I missed it?!"

"You didn't miss anything." He reached out to trail a hand down my arm, watching it as it went.

I probably would've been miserable yesterday anyway, as messed up as I'd been. But I'd gotten sleep now, good, restful, fulfilling sleep.

His gaze came back to mine, and I pulled my fingers out from where they'd curled, moving instead to straddle him. First unbuttoning his jeans, and then unzipping the zipper, I couldn't help the grin that spread across my face.

"All bets are off?" I asked. "Whenever, whatever?"

His breathing slowed, and his voice softened. "The belt is gone for good. We can watch as many sexy movies as you want, sleep in the same bed—naked for all I care—and continue reading hot fairy porn."

He glanced over at my book, and I folded a bit in amusement, before shimmying his jeans and boxers down past his hips. He helped me, scooting a little, and I ran my hands down his skin, starting at the top and ending inside his boxers.

He was ready, and I'd hardly done anything. I guess that's what happens when you stave it off for three months.

Bunching the sides of my dress in his hands, he slowly lifted it above my head, the fabric dangling against my skin and focusing my attention on how it ached for him. My skin alone, primed and ready, waiting. Unclasping my bra, I let it fall to our laps, watching him closely as he took in the sight of me.

That was about all the restraint we had. We fell over each other, hurrying to this new place where there were no longer any barriers in the most indulgent, incessant, and insatiable of ways.

After, I closed my eyes and focused on the length of his body against mine, tried to force out the one nagging thought that kept popping up amid the explosion of contentment and leftover crumbs of pleasure: Lia would hate me for this.

The guilt seeped in as I let my thoughts drift there, but I'd promised myself when I moved here that I would leave her behind, wouldn't speak of her or think of her. Breathing it out, I buried my face in Kai's armpit.

"You okay?" he asked.

"I've never been more okay," I assured him.

"You're shaking. Are you sure you're okay? That was okay?"

"You don't strike me as the type to be unsure of your prowess, Mr. Allen."

"But you're shaking."

"Maybe I'm cold."

"Are you?"

"Sure." I didn't know what I was. I was perfect. And everything after that would have to find a way to fall in line.

He covered me with my quilt anyway, and I contemplated my renewed hope for the future.

A girl shouldn't ask for more.

FALL

18

A Walking Newspaper
Savannah

Today was the day it was all gonna fall into place for me. Some girls would've made the announcement right away, but I wanted to be sure. I'd miscarried before and didn't need to tell everyone, only to have our plan backfire on us.

It was exactly three months now, four if anyone but Andy asked, and safe in the second trimester. So I'd taken the afternoon off to tell everybody, and after swapping work heels for walking shoes, headed to where Andy was working. They were remodeling the church on the corner of Main Street, right behind my duplex.

I checked the scaffolding for him, the fall breeze winding its way up my miniskirt, but found only Georgie. Crossing my fingers Andy hadn't left for lunch, I placed one hand on the stair railing and prepared to enter the church. This place had me nervous since second grade, since I'd run into the priest out front and he'd asked about my mother. I'd had no idea she ever set a foot inside and didn't know what to think after he referred to her by nickname.

Turned out, they'd gone to school together. But he'd been too friendly, acting like he knew me too, as if he had me figured out. I'd stayed far away from priests after that.

Almost thirty years later, and I was still thankful the doors opened before I reached them.

Andy walked out, grinning when he saw me, and I fidgeted a little in the heavy I was about to lay down on him.

"What're you doin here?" he asked, stopping in front of me to scratch his stomach.

"I have something to tell you."

His eyes twinkled. "Are you horny?"

I rolled my eyes, though I had used this on him once before. "No, silly. I'm pregnant."

His grin, smoothing out the puckers on his chin, grew as big as I'd ever seen it. "Well, that sounds like cause for celebration."

"I was hoping you'd say that." I clasped my hands behind my back to make my chest look bigger. It was a nervous habit, thanks to Ma, telling me I needed to appear bigger than I was or I was never going to get a man.

He lifted me up in a hug. "I know I ain't supposed to do this in public, but that's great news, Savannah. Really great news."

"Thanks, Andy. Congrats to you, too."

He let me go. "Congrats to Kai, you mean."

"Right." I kept forgetting that's what we were doing this for. Andy might be my friend now, and a hell of a lover, but I wanted Kai and that house he was building. "We should still celebrate though, don't you think?"

"Why don't you let me take you to lunch," he suggested.

Yeah, that probably made the most sense, but now that he'd mentioned it, I was in the mood. Maybe though, now that there was no longer good reason to have sex with me, maybe he wouldn't want to.

"Or…" He tilted his head closer to mine and lowered his voice. "We could do lunch at your place."

I grinned. "I choose that."

So we headed over to my place, talking about how nice it would be to eat outside on a sunny day like today, planning to eat our sandwiches on the steps. Before we made it to the kitchen, however, we'd torn each other's clothes off. These pregnancy hormones, I could already tell, were really going to give him a run for his money.

When it was over, I made sure to tell him how much sex a pregnant girl needs.

"Really?" he asked.

"Really." I stood up next to him and pulled my panties back on. "So, you up for it?"

"Me?"

"Who else, Andy?" I grabbed his boxers from where he'd tossed them and dropped them in his lap.

He ran a hand up my inner thigh.

"Is that a yes?" I asked.

"Damn right it is," he said.

I looked for my bra.

"Hey," he said from behind me. "Kai's gonna know it's not his. I mean, you haven't had sex with him in three months."

"Four," I corrected, turning to watch him pull jeans over muscled legs. "But I'm three months pregnant and we can lie, say I'm one month more than I am. So don't forget that."

He paused and looked over at me. Well, at my breasts. I stuck them out a bit. "So, you just found out you were pregnant?"

"No, you idiot. I found out two months ago. I'm just telling people now 'cuz it's safe. You aren't supposed to tell anyone until after the first trimester."

"But you kept having sex with me."

"Yeah, and I don't plan to stop."

"Why?"

"Well, until Kai takes me back, what's the point?" I put my bra on and stepped back into my miniskirt. "Besides, if you must know, I like how you touch me."

"Oh, that I know." He winked. "You ain't shy about it."

I made a face and slapped him together a sandwich. He leaned against the island to eat, and I hopped up on the counter next to him.

Halfway through, he stopped chewing. "You like how Kai touches you?"

I shrugged. "Sure." It was like comparing apples to oranges, frankly. Two totally different men.

He bit viciously into the last of his sandwich, and I figured that meant he wanted another, so I padded over to the fridge. He ate the second as fast as he'd eaten the first.

"You want a third?" I asked, this time without getting up.

He shook his head. "Nah, I don't want to eat you out of house and home."

"Well, I better get used to it, if this is a little boy in me."

He slid his enormous feet across the kitchen floor, spread my legs to rest between them, and put a hand over my belly.

"That's my baby in there?" he asked.

"No, it's Kai's baby," I corrected. "And with it, we get what we want."

Resting his forehead against mine, he sighed. Then, with a hard quick kiss, he pulled away and walked to the door.

"Later, Savannah," he yelled on his way out.

"Later, Andy."

I watched him through the window and then made myself a sandwich before heading over to the grocery store.

During the first block, I planned out the baby's room. The second, I decorated the kitchen. I'd been thinking of redoing mine, but it would be more fun to just start over in a new house. Way more fun. The third, I planted a flower bed, and the fourth, I jazzed up what would be our master bedroom.

Tiger print and cherry red. Andy didn't think Kai would mind. We stayed up late one night, going through each room, and Andy said he'd let me do whatever I wanted, if he were Kai. If tiger print and cherry red turned me on, he'd said, he'd do the whole damn house in tiger print and cherry red

That would be tacky, I knew, but it was okay for the bedroom. Anyway, it'd been sweet of him. Who knew? Andy could actually be sweet.

Kai sure as hell hadn't been. But Kai was charming, and sort of funny, and intense like a mystery you couldn't stand not figuring out.

I hadn't figured him out, at least, and it pissed me off to no end that Faryn acted like she actually had.

He was at the service desk when I walked in, and there was no line so I slid along the counter and rang the bell. He looked up, and I greeted his frown with a smile. It was rude, if you asked me, that he didn't even try to hide his irritation.

"Can we talk in your office?" I asked cheerfully, determined not to be derailed.

"No, we can't. I'm busy."

"Not for this you aren't."

He gave me a scathing look and went back to what he was doing.

"Please, Kai?"

"Please what, Savannah?" But he didn't stop.

"Please, can we talk in your office?"

He slapped the pen down. "Is that the same sort of please as 'please put on your fucking clothes and leave my apartment'?"

Okay, I could give him that. "Listen, I'm sorry about that. It wasn't my finest hour."

"Ya think?"

"I can't help what you do to me, Kai. You used to like that."

He rolled his eyes back down to his work and picked up his pen. "Have a nice day, Savannah."

"Kai, please. I really am sorry. That won't happen again."

"Damn right, it won't," he muttered.

I waited for him to look up, to say something, to acknowledge me again. But as long as I stood there, he ignored my existence, and I began to think I really wasn't going to make it back into that office.

So I let out with it. "I'm pregnant."

"Good for you, Savannah." Still though, his eyes were on his work.

"*Four months* pregnant," I whispered.

He froze. "Don't start bullshitting me for attention. I don't have time for that."

"I'm not." I pouted. "I just didn't want to tell you until after the first trimester. I mean, you know what happened before. I wanted to be sure before I ruined your life."

This was where he was supposed to say a baby of mine would never ruin his life. I'd daydreamed he might even go so far as to say Faryn had voodooed his mind, and this was exactly the kind of reason he needed to get away from her.

But he didn't. "Thanks for letting me know," was what he said.

"What?" I cried. "That's it?"

He shushed me. "Please do not make a scene."

"Then take me to your office," I seethed.

"No!" Aghast, as if I'd asked for the fucking moon.

"Yes! Or you'll *get* a scene!"

"Fine." He swung open the half door to let me in and followed me there.

I sat on the chair where we'd once had sex and ran my

fingers along its arms. It was a fond memory.

Ooh, I could use that. "Maybe this right here was where he was conceived."

Kai rolled his eyes. "You have got to be kidding me."

My spine shot up straight. "Of course I'm not kidding you. What do you want me to say? Be careful who you fuck, you might get them pregnant? Well, you weren't too careful I guess, and now I'm fucking pregnant."

He doubled over and placed his palms to the surface of his desk, dropping his head in defeat. "Shit."

"Shit is right." Though, I didn't really feel that way. I'd been trying to get pregnant for five years, ever since my miscarriage.

"Shit!" He picked up his hands and slammed them back down.

I frowned. "So, what are you going to do about it?"

He looked at me, fuming. I shrunk a bit in the chair. "What kind of question is that?" he asked. "You want me to pay to get rid of it?"

"No! I...I mean, like, don't you want to get back together?"

"Why the hell would I want to get back together?"

"Well, because. Faryn's not giving you a baby."

"Have you ever heard me ask for a baby?"

I chewed on my tongue. This wasn't going as well as I'd thought. He actually hadn't ever asked for a baby, and had I thought about this a little more clearly, maybe I should've known this was coming. "You don't want kids, Kai? Ever?"

His sat in his desk chair. "I would've hoped to have them

with a wife, not you."

I put on the smile he used to like so much and leaned forward a bit, as seductively as I could. "I could be your wife, Kai," I cooed.

"You will never be my wife, Savannah."

I slumped back in the chair and crossed my legs with a huff. "Then build me a house."

"Build yourself a house."

"So you're not going to do anything?" I screeched. "I'm on my own?"

"I'll take care of it, of course." He shook his head. "I mean, I'll support it, and I'll be its dad."

"Don't sound so happy about it," I grumbled, crossing my arms and pumping my foot.

"I'm gonna need some time to adjust, okay? Cut me some slack. You've got a few months on me here."

I sighed. He was right. There was still time for him to come around. "Okay, I'm sorry." After a long beat of silence, I stood. "You think about it then, and, well, you know where to find me."

With elbows on the desk and back hunched over, he sank his head deep into his hands and didn't reply.

But it was true, he did know where to find me. And he'd better come around.

I let myself out and headed to my next stop. There was one more person to tell, and I was looking forward to her reaction the most. If Kai wasn't going to break up with Faryn, then maybe I could get Faryn to break up with Kai.

Picturing happy family meals—me, Kai, baby, Uncle

Andy, and my mom—I walked to Chuck's, heading around back to run my hand along his Camaro for good luck. The curves of that car did it for me every time. They'd even clouded my judgment once, that and the alcohol I'd funneled into myself on my twenty-first birthday, and I'd let Chuck have his way with me in it. He'd been twenty-eight and a little less greasy. I'd been excited to have an older man.

Smiling at the memory, I pushed through the back door by the bathrooms and was able to take in Faryn before she saw me. I had to admit, she really was beautiful. I'd never been into girls, but with the pregnancy hormones wiping out my hatred, I almost wanted her myself.

As usual, she hung over the bar next to Lewis, laughing at something he said, and Chuck's nose was in his paper at the other end. Did they do nothing else in here all day? Why had Chuck even hired her full-time? He always hired part-time. Slimeball must have just wanted the eye candy.

I shook my head and wandered over to take a stool, leaving one empty between me and Lewis.

Faryn placed a napkin square in front of me. "Hello, Savannah," she said.

"Hello, Faryn."

"Can I get you something to drink?"

"Pregnant women aren't supposed to drink."

She raised an eyebrow. "Congrats."

I smiled mischievously. "Don't cha wanna know who the daddy is?"

"Not really."

"Kai. Kai's the daddy."

"My ass, Kai's the daddy." She even dared to laugh. "I know where he's been, Savannah, and he hasn't been with you."

She wasn't even concerned, and the smooth porcelain on her face was distracting. I shook my head of it. "I'm four months along, Faryn. I just wanted to be sure it was a healthy pregnancy before I said anything."

The muscles in her jaw twitched, and her brown eyes flashed darkly. She stood up a little straighter and readjusted her shirt, pulling it down so her breasts were more pronounced.

"Maybe if Kai doesn't move me into that house of his, you and I could raise the baby together." I was only half-kidding, half-messing with her. "You ever been with a girl, Faryn?" Then I caught myself. Was she a witch or something?

But I had managed to throw her off. She'd taken a small step back, and her arms were at a loss, crossing, uncrossing, crossing again. Chuck and Lewis stared at me, openmouthed, Lewis with his trademark drool eking out the corner.

"Anyway, I told Kai too, so you don't have to worry about that. But I didn't want to waste any time getting the news to you."

"Well, lookie here," Lewis mumbled. "A walking fucking newspaper."

I glared at him. "Why's everybody always on her side?"

"Because she's nice," he responded, with a snort.

Chuck put his hands up. "I'm all for you getting the girl, Savannah. Hell, you and Faryn get together and you can both work here full-time."

I smiled sweetly at him and then turned that same syrup on the girl in front of me. I'd have to do some thinking on that. Though I'd probably wake up in five more months and only want men again, it was an interesting thought, at least for now.

Seriously, those curves and that glorious head of hair made for some serious fantasy.

I sat there awhile, enjoying it, but since she didn't seem to have any sort of reaction in her whatsoever, I got bored. I would've been up for a fight, or her screaming and crying and running to the bathroom, or her taking me up on my tentative girl-on-girl offer, which was growing less tentative by the minute.

I would've been up for anything really, so it was sort of a letdown that she just stared out past my head like I wasn't even there. But I guess, what could she do? It wasn't my fault I'd had a relationship with Kai before her, and that we fucked our silly brains out and had a baby. It was just life.

So, with a sigh, I stood and headed out back, giving Chuck a look that dared him to follow me for a ride in his Camaro.

19

REVELATIONS

Faryn

After Savannah left, I escaped to the bathroom. Leaning over the sink, arms rigid as they held me up off the counter, I stared at my reflection in the mirror.

All the things I'd been flickered across my face so fast I could hardly recognize myself—child, adult, sister, daughter, mother, friend, lover, business owner.

Which of these labels did I want to hold onto? Which was I meant to be?

Bulbous tears pushed their way out my eyes, and a knock came at the door.

"Faryn?"

It was Kai.

Swiping my cheeks clear, I turned on the faucet to wash my hands, as if I was finishing up instead of getting started. Opening the door, I put on the most relaxed face I could muster.

"They told me Savannah already came by," he said. "I'm so sorry you had to hear it from her."

I didn't say anything, just slid by him and headed back to the bar.

He followed me and cleared his throat, eyeing Chuck and Lewis until Lewis slid off his stool for the bathroom. Chuck waited a beat longer, then huffed and made his way to the depths of the kitchen.

"I came to tell you right away," he said, joining me behind the bar, setting his hip up against it, facing me. "But obviously that wasn't soon enough."

"It's okay, Kai." Holding onto the ridge in front of me, I stared straight ahead, taking a deep breath to keep from exploding into small glass shards of misery. "Life throws curveballs, that's what it does."

"I'm not convinced it's true yet."

"You don't think she's really pregnant?" I guess she had established herself as a liar.

"Or she is, and it isn't mine. Shouldn't she be showing at four months?"

"I don't know, Kai. I don't think necessarily."

"This doesn't change anything. I want you. I choose you."

"I know." But I wasn't so sure it didn't change anything.

"Come take a ride with me?" he asked. "I wanted to bring you out to the house after work anyway."

I didn't know how I felt about this house of his, but I also didn't want to be at work, now that my head was churning. Chuck didn't really need me; the only time he really needed me was on the weekend.

Heading into the kitchen, I leaned my hip on the perpetually-open door frame.

"Chuck?"

He stuck his head inside from the back screen door. It was oddly not like him to give us so much privacy.

"Mind if I take off?"

"Everything okay, Faryn?"

I nodded.

"He's not forcing you? I mean, you want to leave, right? Because you know you can always use me as an excuse, say I won't let you go."

"I know. Thanks, Chuck."

He didn't say anything right away. Then, "So...you want to go?"

"Yes."

He waved his hand at me and went back to his cigarette. I took that for approval.

Lewis was back at the bar and nodded as we passed. Kai pushed the door open, and the crisp air slapped at me a little. This was somewhat needed.

He had his bike today, and as usual made me wear his jacket. I held onto his starched work shirt and rested my cheek on his back, soaking him into me the best I could. The ride was quick, due more to his speed than anything else, and when he stopped on the side of the road, I didn't let go.

I wanted to cry, hold onto him and sob, because I felt like this might be it. This might be the first domino to fall, and it was never a good idea to be in the path of tumbling boulders, no matter how small.

He let me sit there like that, while I swallowed my tears, but he knew everyone working on the house, and they were watching us. Forcing myself to hop off, I wrapped his jacket tighter around me. It was September, and September had a bite to it.

Thanks to his years in the construction business, Kai knew exactly who he wanted doing what. This meant it wasn't going as quickly as it might have, had he just gone with the people available. Today, the house sat undecided, half frame and half shell.

We walked through what would someday be the front door and sat down where he might someday put a kitchen table.

Cross-legged, we faced each other with our knees touching.

"You're going to get your khakis dirty," I told him.

"How are you feeling about this Savannah thing?" he asked.

I looked at his belt—not the one he'd worn the first three months of our relationship. "I don't know. It's probably for the best, I guess."

"What does that mean?"

I sighed. This was it. This was where it was all going to flow out, my past into the present. I tried to prepare myself. "You want a house."

"Yeah." He wrinkled his forehead. "I'm not sure what

you're getting at."

"Most people who want houses also want something to put inside their house. Like a family."

"Okay. Do you have something against families?"

"I don't want kids, Kai."

"Not at all?"

I shook my head.

"Not ever?"

"No."

"Not even with me?"

I winced, unable to make that definitive, as it might wound him. If there was anyone I'd consider having kids with, it was him, but... "I just don't think I could do it again."

"Do it *again*?"

I looked straight at him, shaky but holding strong. "They weren't my own. I didn't take off and leave my own kids or anything."

He sat silent, confused, waiting for more. I could tell he was withholding judgment and made a mental note to thank him for that later.

Staring levelly into his eyes, I readied myself to say it out loud—which would only make real what I'd left behind, what I'd lost, what I'd lived. "I raised my sister and brothers, four of them. Finnegan was eight when I had to take over, Fletcher seven, Foster six, and Frankie four. Frankie's the girl— Francine. Four kids is a lot of work, especially for a nineteen-year-old."

He was stone. Digesting perhaps? Or maybe horrified I hadn't shared this before.

I reached out and took his hand, gave it a little shake. He blinked. "You raised four kids on your own?"

"Pretty much."

"Why? What happened to your parents?"

I gulped down the solid knot of metal that rose in my throat. "Well, one day I was livin' it up, sort of Savannah and Andy style, fighting with my parents about college and being altogether an irresponsible brat, and the next day they were gone." My hands trembled, but Kai wrapped them tightly in his. I closed my eyes to continue. "It was a car accident. One minute I was coasting along and the next I was complete authority over a house, a business, and a family. It was overnight, Kai, it was..."

I let what it was sit there between us unspoken. It had been a lot of things, and a few more I couldn't even explain. I opened my eyes.

"Fuck," he commented softly.

My shoulders slumped, and I let my hair fall, creating a shield. "It was difficult. Very. And I wouldn't trade it. But never being able to find my own way, or grow up at my own pace, or shirk any of that responsibility? At nineteen, it was stifling. I felt like I was choking on my own sanity so many times, and I often dreamt of getting away. I did what I had to do, for them, and then they were grown up. The less they needed me, the more I itched to get out. I tried to deal with it, to get past it, but that didn't work. When it got so bad I could hardly think straight, I left."

"I'm so sorry, Faryn." He brushed the hair out of my face. "I'm sorry about your parents, and I'm sorry that happened to you."

We were silent a moment.

"Savannah is so not what you bargained for," he finally muttered.

"I didn't bargain for you, either, Kai, and I wouldn't trade that for the world. Even if she comes along with it."

He unclasped our hands and scooted around behind me, legs on either side of mine and arms tight around my torso. I pulled my legs up and twisted a little so I could still see his face.

"Were you ever planning on going back?" he whispered.

"I was hoping to."

"And now?" These words came out as if he'd scraped them against sandpaper. He cleared his throat. "Are you still hoping to?"

"I don't plan on leaving you, Kai." I rested my head in his neck. "Besides, I like it here, I like this life. But maybe…"

"Maybe what?"

"Maybe that would be better for you, if I did leave."

"Why the hell would you think that'd be better for me?" His panic danced with anger, and I nuzzled his neck to soothe him.

"You could have a family, with Savannah and your baby," I explained. "Maybe that's best."

"No matter what happens with you, Savannah will not live in this house."

I closed my eyes. It was what I wanted to hear, of course, even if I'd already known it, but I was also afraid I'd let him down. Maybe what he wanted out of life was more in line with what Savannah wanted, than what I did.

"Interesting that we were both forced into the family business," he commented. "What was it, what'd you do?"

"Kennels, vet clinics, that kind of thing. My dad was a vet and my mom an amazing businesswoman. We own the city pretty much. The county, really."

He looked impressed. Yes, we'd made a lot of money. But money didn't matter.

"It's very dirty work," I assured, so he wouldn't feel so impotent in the face of my past success. Success also meant nothing. "Imagine all the dog shit, for starters."

"Still, you were probably in some high corner office somewhere, coordinating it all."

It was all glass, too. I'd loved it, but he didn't need to know that. "I tried to spend a day or two a week at one place or the other, so I didn't lose touch. Anyway, can we talk about this some other time?"

He kissed my cheek, pressed his head against mine. "Of course, I'm sorry. It hurts?"

"Every day."

"It must be harder, losing your parents like that, than having one walk away from you and knowing they made the choice."

"I would think it would be harder for you," I said.

"But I can hate her for it, where you have no one to direct your anger at."

I didn't want to talk about me, and who I had to direct my anger at. I could only sit inside these memories for too long before they overtook me. "Do you know where your mom went?" I asked.

"Back to Hawaii. My dad used to say it was the mainland she couldn't handle, the cold weather, but I knew it was him. I knew he drove her away. He'd drive anyone away."

We fell silent, and I realized all the workers had gone home for the night. When had that happened?

"I don't want to drive you away," he finally whispered.

"I'm not going anywhere," I said.

"But I can't have you and a family, can I? Or maybe what I'm really asking is, I can't have a family *with* you. And wanting that—or talking about it too much—would drive you away."

I didn't say anything.

"I want what I didn't have. I want to be a part of a family unit, a good one, even if it's from the other side. I figure I have the control now, and can make it what I want it to be. But you are the most important component of that, so if we stop at us, I'll deal with that."

"I don't want you to have to deal with anything because of me."

"Faryn, we are more than I ever thought I'd find, more than I even believed existed. And if I'm not meant for the rest of it, I'm good with that. All I need is you by my side."

My insides swelled, every bit of them, and I sank further against him.

We sat inside his future home, dreaming perhaps of different things, until the sky began to deepen. Then he silently pulled me up and led me back to his bike to drive me home.

I let him walk me up the stairs, but stopped him in front of my apartment.

"I'm not leaving you alone," he said, shaking his head. "I won't leave you alone."

"I'll be fine, Kai. Nothing's happened in ages. And I need some time to wrap my head around this whole baby thing— what you want, and what I can or will or won't do about it."

"I told you, Faryn. I don't need the family. I just need you."

"I won't let you give something like that up for me. That's huge. Wanting kids—or not wanting them—can ruin relationships."

"Nothing will ruin us. I won't let anything ruin us."

"Let's say we don't have kids and live happily ever after. There's still this baby. What about this baby? I can't be the mean stepmother that doesn't give a crap. It doesn't work like that. *I* don't work like that."

"But there might not even be a baby," he reminded. "So can't we wait until we know for sure? Can't we forget about it until there's proof?"

"One night to think, okay?" I stood a little straighter, needing everything I had to deliver this to his beautifully saddened face. "With you here, well, you're all I can see and nothing else matters, and I don't think that's healthy."

"One night?" he asked.

I nodded.

"Okay, but I'm coming back early, before work."

"Okay."

He pulled me to him and kissed me fiercely, the veracity

bottoming out to a genuine tenderness that sent bolts of aching right through me. I opened my eyes as his body moved away, his lips the last to go, and watched as he disappeared down the stairs.

20

DESPERATELY UNREQUITED

. . .

After Kai left and Faryn fell asleep, I moved from my hiding space to collect the leaves that had fallen from the trees.

There was something about crisping autumn leaves that resonated with me, and in that, I found their beauty. If you looked hard enough you could find one in about every color, but I was going for the dead today.

It was how I felt inside, curled up, dried, and twisted.

And I wanted everyone to know it.

Well, Faryn at least. She needed to know what she was doing to me.

I got back into her apartment, easy when you had a key, and set the leaves down on the white tiles of the kitchen countertop.

Knowing, as I already did, where everything was, I carefully and quietly knelt down and reached far into the lowest cupboard for the canning jars that predated Faryn's arrival. There were a lot of windows in the living room, and I wanted one for each. Settling on the kitchen floor, I welcomed the cool temperature of the white and black tile.

White and black, like Faryn and me. I was black inside, burnt and filled with ashes, and I would not let her, in her innocent angelic glory, ignore me any longer.

After stuffing a handful of leaves inside each jar, I carried them one by one to the living room. I was tempted to open the windows, so she'd know she couldn't keep me out any longer, but was already chilled through myself.

Scattering the few remaining leaves along the sill, I sat on the couch and admired my work. The couch smelled like Kai, an odor I knew all too well at this point, and it sort of made me sick to my stomach. Standing when I couldn't take it any longer, I snuck into Faryn's room and sat on her bed, careful not to rouse her.

They say people are attracted to those who look like them, which is sort of sick and completely narcissistic, but I couldn't completely disagree. I'd noticed it, oddly, time and time again, so what did she see in Kai? They looked nothing alike. Anyway, I knew more than he did. I knew everything. And in that knowledge I was certain they weren't meant to be together. She, and her face, belonged to me, as I belonged to her. We were one. Or at least, we would be soon.

It was becoming increasingly obvious to me that there

wasn't any room for Kai in this equation, and unfortunately for him, there wasn't anything I wouldn't do in order to make sure things turned out in my favor.

I didn't want to hurt her, but if she kept on this trajectory—speeding away from me—well, I wasn't sure I'd have a choice. If only she would choose me on her own, what I wanted, what I needed. If only she could see, without me making her see.

She slept soundly, but I figured not for long. Always, she sensed when I was here.

I waited for it, for her to remember me, always before slipping away I would wait, and it never failed. Taken hold of by her fear, by her sense of me, she tossed and turned, whimpered and whined.

"Yes," I whispered. "Yes, I'm here."

Of course I wanted her happy, as you always do of someone you love, but I was starting to prefer it this way. The torment meant I was making a dent in her otherwise Kai-filled psyche.

The torment meant she was starting to understand.

21

WINDOWSILL OFFERINGS

Kai

Knowing I wouldn't be able to concentrate until I'd made sure Faryn was safe and sound and had a good night's sleep, I woke up early to head over to her place.

She didn't respond to me pounding down her door, so I let myself in and shot straight for the bedroom. Asleep but crying, she was clutching her nightgown so tight her knuckles were white, the sheet twisted around her leg and the comforter thrown off the bed.

I unwound the sheet, a feat greater than I would have thought possible, and pulled her up in my arms.

Clasping her fist in my hand and kneading at her fingers to loosen them, I shushed her as best I could. It broke me though, seeing it, what she'd dealt with all those weeks before she'd said anything. And it broke me twice that I'd let her down, that I hadn't been here, that I'd let her talk me into leaving her. One night was all it had taken, one night and she was a mess.

I often woke in the night to check on her, and I'd always found her peaceful, sometimes even with a faint smile. Whenever I'd touched her, she'd responded by curling against me. But now, wrapped tightly in my arms, she hardly noticed anything outside of what was happening in her head.

"Faryn," I urged, wiping her tears. "Faryn, wake up."

With a shudder, her eyes popped open. But they weren't the eyes I knew. They were hard, feral like a wild animal's. She jumped away from me, clasping the same rigid fingers to her head that she'd had around the sheet.

After pounding a fist into her thigh twice, three times, she flew to the bathroom, slammed the door, and crumpled to the floor. I knew because I heard her land.

Obviously, she wanted a minute, so I waited a bit before following.

Resting my shoulder on the door, I let my head fall against it and tapped the wood with my fingertip. "Faryn?"

When she didn't respond, I turned the knob, but it didn't budge.

She'd locked me out.

She'd locked me out? Could she honestly want me to go?

Minutes passed, and I didn't know what to do. I tried to leave a few times, but ultimately couldn't leave her alone like this. Tried sitting on the couch, but had a hard time staying still. Almost knocked again, but she knew I was here.

I settled for pacing the short hall, even though it made me anxious, like a caged beast, and soon after I heard the lock unclick. I waited for her to open the door wide, but when she didn't, I did it myself. Leaning back against the tub, she had her knees propped up in front of her. A barrier.

I crouched down. "Baby, it's okay. It's just me."

"I know. I'm sorry."

"I'm not doing that again. If you need space, I'll sleep on the couch."

She nodded, letting out one final sob before pulling herself together.

I took a crunchy brown leaf from her hair. "Come lay on the couch," I suggested. "I'll stay long enough for you to get a good nap, okay?"

She didn't respond, probably not too keen on the idea of sleep about now. But she needed it, and I hoped waking up after a more peaceful rest might cancel out how she felt right then. I tugged at her, and she let me guide her along, until we were situated on the couch the way we'd been many times before.

That was when I noticed the windowsills—dead leaves and canning jars, an odd choice.

"Did you put those there?" I asked.

"What?"

"Those dead leaves." My entire body coiled in apprehension, and no longer was I simply regretful that I'd left her, but also terrified she hadn't been alone. "Did you put those there?"

She took her time sitting up. "No."

"You're sure?"

"Of course I'm not sure," she snapped. "But who's ever heard of decorating for fall like that?"

"*Fuck!*" I cried, running my hand through my hair. "Whoever did this knew I wasn't here, knew this was the one night I didn't stay." I eyed the remnants of leaves on her pajamas and felt like I'd been punched in the gut, hard. "And they were in your room. On you, over you, something." What sonofabitch had been that close to her? So help me, I would fucking kill him.

She folded her arms across her chest, and we stared at the menacing glass jars with growing unease. Growing until it raged in me, and when I couldn't take it anymore, I grabbed the garbage can from the kitchen and tossed them all in. Marching the bag downstairs, I threw it in the trash Leon kept outside.

When I got back, the fury working its way inside me paused, as I was struck with how small and broken she appeared, sitting curled up on that couch. She needed me to be comforting and logical, instead of a crazy fucking lunatic.

Sitting on the coffee table in front of her, I clasped my hands and set my elbows to my knees. It was the best position I knew, to hold myself together. "Who does this eliminate?" I asked. "Your fiancé?"

"Ex," she corrected.

"If he were watching us that closely, someone would have noticed a stranger in town. So it's Leon, Lewis or Chuck? But Philip's the creepiest of them all, except the L wouldn't make sense for him." I thought about this, about what I could *do,* instead of who my fists could find reason to pummel. "Maybe I should confront them, see how they react."

"What if it's a girl?" Faryn asked. "Or what if it's Andy?"

"Why would it be a girl? And why would it be Andy?"

She shrugged.

Why would she think of Andy? Though, Andy was stupid. Who knew what he might have done. "What'd Andy do?" I wondered.

"Savannah hit on me yesterday at the bar," she said, instead of answering my question.

"What?"

"Savannah hit on me yesterday at the bar, when she told me she was pregnant with your baby. She hit on me."

"Little Savvy Lane, we used to call her. Little for short. I guess it's possible." Was there anyone it couldn't be? This possibility only drove my rage harder, and I had to close my eyes to keep it under control. When I spoke, I had to actually think about loosening my jaw. It was tight, angry, and I wanted to rip this SOB's ear off. "What did Andy do?" I asked again.

She sighed. "He came over one night to talk, about how you guys aren't really best friends anymore."

"I'm still his best friend."

"Well, not the kind he wants. Not the kind that gets drunk with him on a regular basis. Not the kind that isn't tied down to a girl."

I narrowed my eyes. "Was he rough with you? I will fucking kill him if he was rough with you." All I wanted at that moment was one stupid reason to annihilate somebody. I didn't care who, I didn't care why. I just cared that I could beat this out on a person who barely deserved it. Which was pretty impressive, that I wasn't simply going for the nearest irritation.

Her eyes slid to the floor. "He was confused. Anyway, I doubt it's him. He just, makes me uncomfortable for some reason. I don't know why."

He made a lot of girls uncomfortable. I shook my head and then my hands, which were squeezed together so tight my fingers had gone numb. To loosen them, and still hurt something, I dug them into my skull.

"I'm sorry," I muttered. "I shouldn't take my frustration out on you. You have enough to deal with as it is." Except, come to think of it, why wasn't she as pissed off as I? Did she not fucking care that someone could've raped and cut her up the night before? I let go of my head, forcing my fists together, and looked up. "Though, you're doing a marvelously better job than I am."

"I'm a mess, Kai. I've just been working on my poker face for a very long time."

Between flashes of rage, I was able to see it again, like when I'd first come back inside after removing all the jars. Her eyelids were puffy and round, her bottom lip bit up and split open, hair in snarls when it was normally brushed smooth. The collar of her t-shirt was still drying from her tears, and her finger twisted itself around the leg of her pajama pants so tight the tip was purple. She was worn, defeated and deflated, more than half-empty.

Scooting to sit next to her, I put an arm around her, and pulled her against me, determined to keep her safe. "I'll sleep on the couch tonight, okay, if you still need time to think? But don't ask me to leave you again because I won't."

She rested her head at my collarbone, and her breath leaked out on my skin. "Just move in," she whispered. "Never leave me. I don't care about anything else anymore."

I lifted her head and looked into the murky depths of her brown eyes, tempted to ask if that included the babies and everything else we'd talked about the day before. But I wasn't going to push my luck, and *never leave me* was dancing repeatedly, and quite fucking ecstatic-like, through my head.

So loudly in fact, I might not have been able to talk if I tried.

22

HUNTING
Kai

I texted my assistant manager to let him know I might not be in until later that afternoon, let Faryn sleep on my lap until she needed to get up for work, and planned my rounds.

Leon worked very early, so he would be first, then Lewis and Chuck, Philip, and maybe I'd finish up with Savannah. Really though, I wasn't taking her too seriously.

I twiddled my thumbs while Faryn showered and bounced my knee under the table while she ate. We walked out together, and I turned back when she crossed the street, waiting until she disappeared inside Chuck's before knocking at Leon's.

There was some movement and other general shuffling

before he made it to the door. His hangdog face greeted me with as much of a smile as he could muster, and I held out one of the glass jars I'd pulled back out of the garbage. This was my strategy, to read their expressions when faced with undeniable evidence.

Leon furrowed his brow and linked his thumbs inside his suspenders. "Mornin', Kai," he said. "Whatcha sellin'?"

My eyes didn't leave his face. "This isn't yours?"

He studied it. "Do I look like the type of guy to can jam?"

I glanced behind me toward the bar, where Faryn was, then at his old limo and back to him. He was an odd duck and sad as a poor dirty bastard, but he did seem to have a heart of gold. Not to mention, he'd never made one inappropriate comment in Faryn's direction. They were friends, maybe even good ones, and he'd never been known as the obsessive type.

"Listen, Leon, someone's been messing with Faryn, and I'm trying to figure out who it is. If you see anything—or anyone—on this property, you'll let me know?"

His eyebrow twitched. "This about Andy?"

"What do you mean, about Andy?"

"Well, I was watchin' TV one night and heard Faryn screamin', so I came out to see what was goin' on and Andy was all over her. It looked like they mighta been talkin' or something, sittin' on the steps like they were, but by the time I got there, he was suckin' her face."

"I'm sorry, can you say that again?" Not that I really needed him to, but how the fuck had I not heard about this? And how the fuck had my lowlife, sonofabitch, supposed best friend thought he could get away with that?

"I was watchin' TV-"

Putting my hand up to stop him, I shook my head of the red buzz threatening my senses. As much as I wanted to give in and beat the ever-loving-shit out of Andy, if I was going to get to the bottom of this, I needed full mental capacity. "So then what happened?"

"I pulled him off her, and she flew up the stairs. I told him if he didn't get the hell outta here, I'd call you."

I about choked, thinking of what might have happened had he not been there. "Thanks, Leon." It took all I had to get these words out, tight as my jaw was.

"Yeah, man. Anytime."

"Did you talk to her after? Was she all right?"

"Like I said, she ran up to her apartment. He came back a little later, all poundin' on her door and swearin' that he'd kill her and stuff. She was yellin' back, but I couldn't hear what she was sayin'. Then he took off and I ain't seen him around since."

The uncontainable anger I'd been friendly with in my twenties took over for a moment, and I fisted my hands at my sides to keep from going after Leon, just because he was the closest available punching bag.

He eyed me while I struggled, even took a step back. When I was finally able to wrap one hand around it, I spun on my heel and marched across the street. Because why had Faryn kept this from me?

As I threw open the door, I realized it would be stupid to waste the element of surprise, so I slammed the jar on the bar and decided to take care of Chuck and Lewis first.

It was a huge testament to my growth and maturity that I was able to make any sort of decision at all, what with the ire coursing through me.

Lewis was unaffected, swiping chin to shoulder to wipe off some drool and then scratching his nub.

Right, the handicap.

Not to mention he was a hundred years old. Both of which would make him a less than stellar stalker. And as much as he appreciated Faryn for every beautiful thing about her, he did it with respect. They, too, were friends, and if I were being honest—not colored by a jealous blinding rage—he looked at her like he might look at a granddaughter.

Chuck, on the other hand, was tense. Now, he'd seen me worked up like this many times in the past, and it usually resulted in me breaking something or getting physically thrown out on the street. But still, if he hadn't done anything wrong, maybe he shouldn't be so fucking fidgety.

I picked up the jar only to slam it back down, and Faryn jumped. The angel on Chuck's neck twitched as his tendons clenched and released. He was trying to stare me down, but ultimately he was a pussy. I had always intimidated him.

"Either one of you see this before?" I asked through bared teeth.

"My mom used to make pickles," Lewis nodded. "Them were good pickles."

Chuck's anxiety was melting to confusion. "Everybody's seen a Ball jar before, Kai. What the hell's gotten into you?"

I pushed my face into his. He backed up. "You been

messin' with Faryn?" I asked.

"That'd be sexual harassment," he noted. "I might be a little flirty, but I'm not into sexual harassment."

"Pretty sure you're into sexual harassment," Faryn muttered. "Not that I think you mean it that way exactly, but if you ever hire someone else, you should probably be a little more careful." Then she looked at me. "Please calm down, Kai. You're kind of freaking me out."

Unclenching my fists, I laid my palms on the bar, stretching my arms out and bending over. Deep breaths. Deep breaths could help me now.

When I had myself leashed back up again, I raised my head. Faryn and Chuck stood on the other side of the bar in what felt like solidarity: the meek and levelheaded versus me, the roaring tyrant. "I'm not talking about what you do around here, Lover Boy." I paused to give him the look that generally put people on their knees. "I'm talking about her apartment, about her personal life."

"I don't know what you're talking about. But if you don't cool it with the windup, I'm going to have to physically remove you from my establishment." He puffed up his chest and glanced at Faryn, who he was obviously using the big words for.

"Fuckin' try me. That ever work for you before?" He'd always needed an army to get me out that door. Then I turned to Faryn. "You lied to me about Andy."

"What?"

"Andy!" I shouted. "You said he came over to talk to you, to cry on your shoulder, but Leon just told me how it went down. He laid his fucking hands on you, and you protected him? Why the hell would you do that?"

"He's your best friend, Kai. And it wasn't like that. He was just confused."

"Screaming and pounding on your door doesn't sound like confused. He threatened you. And after all this shit went down, you still didn't tell me." It was fucking unbelievable.

She readjusted, straightening her back a bit and furrowing her brow. "That's not quite how it happened, Kai."

"Why are you covering for him?" I yelled. "He's a fucking scoundrel! I should know! I trained him!"

She frowned. "So you're a fucking scoundrel now?"

My temperature cooled in the wake of hearing that word come out of her mouth. She never swore, and it rode out cold. My shoulders dropped, and I pounded the bar with both fists, but weakly. "I used to be."

"Well, then maybe Andy used to be, too." She took a step forward. "I didn't tell you because I didn't think it was worth ruining your friendship. So what if he tried to kiss me? He was confused and upset. I took his best friend from him, and he wanted you back. Maybe he thought I'd be a loser's trophy or something, or maybe he was just plain mad at me. Ultimately, he was hurting, and I got out unscathed, so it didn't matter."

I shook my arms out. "I'm sorry, Faryn. I'm out of my mind. I can't help it."

"I know, I just don't think you should be charging around like this. It's not going to do anyone any good."

Chuck crossed his arms and stormed into the kitchen, then out the back door with a slam. He was first on my list now, the only one for sure still on it. Faryn placed her hands on my face and pulled my attention back to her. She ran her small thumbs along my cheeks and kissed me like a whisper on my lips.

"Don't you have to work today?" she asked.

"This is top priority," I answered.

She sighed and released me. "Don't ruin your life because of me, Kai. Don't screw up your job."

"I about own that place, Faryn. And I should hope Mike can handle a day without me."

Backing up again, she frowned.

"I just need to talk to Andy, and I'll be on my way."

"Does this mean you'll be home late?"

I faltered in her phrasing: home. "No. I'll be home on time." Her safety was far more important than anything else. "In fact, I'll meet you here." I looked to Lewis. "You'll keep an eye on her until I get back?"

He nodded. "But is somebody gonna tell me what's going on?"

"Later, Lewis. Let's not get Kai started again, shall we?"

They shared a look, and I turned, grumbling as I walked out. Fucking Andy.

He was at the old church, and I about broke the door down on my way in. It took everything I had not to throw the glass jar at his face from across the room. I reveled in the thought for a moment, how it might splinter and mar him more for the bastard he was.

"You want a piece of my girlfriend?" I asked, approaching briskly and shoving the jar into his stomach.

He oomphed out a gust of air and grabbed hold of it. "No, I don't."

"Then why'd you try to take one?"

"What are you talking about?" he snapped.

"The way I hear it, you damn near attacked her."

"She fucking nark on me?"

For that I punched him, just once. His nose was ugly to begin with.

"Fuck, Kai!" he cried, looking like he might come back with something, if he weren't holding a glass jar in one hand and his bleeding nose in the other. Plus there was the issue of his obvious guilt, which, if he gave me a reason, I'd be happy to shove down his damn throat. "I knew that bitch was shifty."

"You want another one, Andy? I not hit you hard enough the first time?"

He didn't say anything.

"It was Leon that narked on you, not Faryn. What I want to know is why the hell you did it and what the fuck you were thinking."

He started to apologize, but I didn't want to hear it. I was so fed up I might blow this entire church apart if I stayed too long. "You come near her again, and I will take your head off. Do you understand?"

His rapid apologies turned to nods, and my muscles locked tight as I tasted in my throat the satisfaction I knew would come if I punched him, or shoved him, or kicked his head in. But Faryn wouldn't want that, and that wasn't me anymore.

"You seen that before?" I nodded at the jar through clenched teeth. The jaw lock was necessary to keep all my urges inside.

He held up his hand and shrugged. "Savannah's got some with candles in 'em."

So I snatched it back and off to Savannah I went.

"You switching teams?" I asked, before she even lifted her gaze up from her desk.

She pushed her lips out. "Wow, Faryn's quite a tattletale, isn't she?"

I put the glass jar on her desk. "This yours?"

"No. Why would I put dead leaves in a glass jar?" Wrinkling her nose, she added, "That's just dirty."

I slid it to the side. "What's going on, Savannah? You really hit on Faryn yesterday?"

She shrugged. "These pregnancy hormones are insanity. I'd take you out back right now and screw your brains out, no strings attached."

"You have a thing for her? You been messing with her?"

She snorted out a laugh. "You think we've been sneaking around behind your back? That's so hot. But sorry, she wasn't interested. If she's cheating on you, I'd finger Chuck for it. His pants are H-A-R-D for her."

"She's not cheating on me," I said, suddenly beyond exhausted. Resting my elbow on the high counter, I ran my hand through my hair and wondered how much to divulge. Who the hell could it be? "You're not trying to scare her or anything?" I asked to make sure.

"Why would I scare her? First, I'd just beat her up. Second, she ain't carrying your baby. I already won."

"Hardly."

She scoffed. "Whatever. You're tied to me for life now. There's no getting around that."

"But you're not tied to her," I pointed out. "Maybe you want us both."

"Maybe, but I wouldn't even know the first way to go about getting her. And really, I don't care all that much."

"Don't you?" I narrowed my eyes, as much as I had the energy for.

She rolled hers. "You're like speaking in tongues or something. Stop wasting my time." On a second thought that put a glint in her eyes, she added, "Unless you plan to make it worth my while, if you know what I mean."

Ugh. How had I been attracted to such an overtly sexual woman like that? The way she presented herself for the taking? Such blatant innuendo now turned my stomach.

Faryn had flipped me upside down.

I waved my hand at Savannah, declining her offer. "I'll leave. I'm going."

Already only a few blocks from the store, I went to work and carried on with my day, forgetting all about Philip until he walked past the service counter with a case of canning jars in his cart.

One look at those and I flew over the counter to strangle him. Mike, thankfully, happened to be walking by. He stopped me from doing any real damage, which I was pretty fucking sure I would've done. Good thing Mike was as big and burly as they came.

"It's nice to see you, Kai," Philip said, amidst a serious case of the shakes. I might have been satisfied if he'd pissed his pants, but no such luck. "It's nice to see you," he repeated.

"Give it up, Philip, you've been sneaking into Faryn's apartment, haven't you?" And then a gasp came. "You have a fucking key!"

Mike still had a hold of my arm, or I would have swung at him.

Philip wiped his face and stepped back, nearly tripping with fear.

Damn straight.

"Of course I haven't been sneaking into her apartment," he stuttered. "Of course not."

I nodded toward his cart. "You recently run out of canning jars, *Philp*? You big on canning?"

He looked into the basket, then back up at me like I was the crazy one. Had he ever looked in a fucking mirror? What grown man had permed hair halfway to their waist? Not to mention feathered sideburns. "It's for my daughter's wedding," he explained.

His daughter was, in fact, getting married. This I knew.

"I wanted to do something," he added. "So she said I could buy supplies. They're gonna make candles with these for the middle of the tables. You know, pretty it up."

Chewing on this, I shrugged Mike off. He double-checked that I had control of myself before leaving. I must have played convincing well enough.

"I'm really sorry if I did somethin' to upset you," Philip said. "It's always nice to see you though."

"Yeah, always nice to see Faryn too, isn't it?"

"Well, sure. Of course it is. She's a real pretty lady, Kai. I ain't denyin' that."

I crossed my arms and stared him down, hoping the tremor of my anger would shake him loose, if there was anything to be revealed.

But he only ducked his head a bit and went on and on about his daughter's wedding. When I couldn't take it any more, I simply walked away, his cries of how nice it was to see me following behind.

Locking myself in my office, I hung my head in my hands. I was no closer to knowing who was messing with Faryn and had no real plan on how to deal with it.

I contemplated calling the cops, but the cops in this town would take one look at Faryn and start stalking her themselves. I didn't trust any of them, and that wasn't only because I used to be the biggest problem they had. Regardless of my past and how shitty they'd treated me—sometimes justifiably and sometimes not—I'd known them my whole life and they were assholes. This was fact.

I had no one to turn to, no one I trusted, and I knew what everyone would say anyway. My dad, for instance, would tell me to get a gun. I'd always thought that was a coward's way out, for people afraid to get up close and personal and hash their shit out. Fists were more therapeutic, less deadly, and made a stronger point.

But this SOB had so far been careful not to get near me, and if I didn't know who he was, I couldn't get near him, so where did that leave me?

It left me thinking maybe a gun wasn't such a bad idea after all.

23

Armed

Kai

I had a hard time taking her clothes off that night, after the day I'd had. I couldn't think of Andy without every muscle in my body reacting, and no matter what I did, those damn jars wouldn't leave my head.

It didn't help that I was now spooked about someone watching us, which felt like spiders on my back.

Even so, it was hard not to watch as she did it for me— slipping her shirt off, curling her leg around mine, weaving her hand down my chest, across my hipbone, low into my boxers...well, she had me there.

I was a man, after all, and definitely fit the stereotypes in this category.

Helping her along the rest of the way, situating her on top of me, bringing her to the edge—watching her there drove me mad.

If only my brain would shut up. Now I knew how women felt, their thoughts going on and on, distracting them from the matter at hand. I'd had plenty of chicks stop me, or slow me down with questions about our relationship, or what I'd meant when I'd said some inane comment that meant nothing, which they'd taken to mean everything.

Women weren't bent on a good time when they were worried about something. It was fact. So how come Faryn was as into this as ever?

Had she forgotten what my day had been like? That we were hunting down a threat to her well-being? I couldn't have forgotten about those damn jars if someone had knocked me senseless.

A thought struck me suddenly, while inside her. "Do you know who it is?" Was that why she was so unconcerned?

Slowing, she lifted her head up a little. "What?"

"Do you know who it is?" I repeated, resting my hands on the crook of her hips to keep her still.

"Of course I don't. Why would you think that?"

Her hair, loose around her face, tickled my skin. It was distracting. *She* was distracting, naked and on top of me. What were we talking about? Oh yeah. "You don't seem worried."

"Can we talk about this later? I'm trying to create some stars right now, for both of us." She looked down to where we were joined. "Are you not into this?"

I tilted her face back to mine, reached my lips to hers, and determined to put it aside for a moment. I would be here, with her, taking and drinking her in.

After, with her collapsed empty on top of me, I kissed her shoulder, ran my palms up and down her back.

The movement felt frantic even to me. Frantic because Savannah had planted a seed, with her talk of them carrying on behind my back, and maybe that was how Faryn knew who it was, if indeed she did.

"I'm still who you want?" I asked, forcing my hands still. "You're still into me?"

Scooting down a bit, she burrowed her head to kiss my neck. "I can't imagine," she momentarily paused for another, "how it would be possible," and another, "for me...to not...be into you."

"There's no one else?"

Rolling off me, she propped up on her elbow. "Excuse me?"

I ran my hand over my face, hoping I hadn't ruined anything by doubting her. "Savannah suggested you might be cheating on me. The possibility of me getting what I deserve has been eating me alive ever since."

No response, but she gazed out the window. It was raining, and the reflection washed down her face in streaks.

"Faryn?"

"You think I'm cheating on you, and that it's my other lover doing all this stuff." Her tone was flat.

"I don't think you're cheating on me-"

"Good." She sent an irritated expression in my direction.

"Because frankly, I'm not sure when I'd have the time."

I'd used this line before, and what I'd quite bitterly meant when I'd used it was that I'd had no space inside the relationship to find an actual minute.

If that wasn't a swift kick in the nuts, being on the other side.

"Am I suffocating you?" I was not a controlling freak of a boyfriend. I was simply trying to keep her safe. Did she not see that?

Her irritation softened, and she sighed. "Of course not, but really, when would I have the time?"

Well, I could think of all the hours she was at work without me for one. And the Camaro, that was always primed and waiting, for two.

"You really think I could do that?" she asked. "That I could love you so completely like I do, every minute of every day, and then turn around and screw someone else?"

I didn't deserve to have her heart in its entirety, this I knew. After what I'd done in my life, I didn't deserve anyone's heart, not even a partial. But aside from that, no, I didn't think she could do that.

"I don't deserve for you to love me like that," I admitted.

Cupping a hand to my face, she ran a thumb across my lips. "Of course you do."

Almost, almost I took her again. A year ago, I would've. Tonight though, my mind rushed ahead. "How can you not be scared, or worried, or at the very least thinking about it?"

She frowned. "I am scared, Kai, but being with you makes me feel safe, makes me forget about it for a little while.

What's wrong with pretending everything's perfect in the few moments I can?"

"What's wrong is he won't be okay watching you forever. He'll catch you off guard, if you're not careful. You have to be careful. We have to be vigilant."

"Are you saying we shouldn't make love anymore?"

"Of course not."

She pressed her body up against mine. "You sure? 'Cuz that's what it sounds like."

"Damnit, Faryn! This is exactly what I'm talking about!"

We stared at each other a moment, a test. But I was damn serious and wasn't going to back down or smile like she was being cute or something.

Eventually, she lay flat and stared out the window, into the stormy night. "This isn't the first time it's happened to me, Kai. Maybe that's why. Maybe I'm used to it."

"What?" I clipped, turning to face her.

"I've been hoping it's unrelated."

"Hoping? And you haven't mentioned it? First you keep Andy from me and now this? What the hell else is there?"

"Nothing, there's nothing else."

I dropped onto my back, and we lay side by side, stiff and awkward like a one-night stand. Was Andy right? Was she shifty? How much else had she kept from me? And did I want to fight about that right now too, on top of everything else?

"Was it Spencer?" I finally asked.

"No," she replied tightly. "Spencer thinks I'm crazy."

"I'm not sure that would matter. I know more than a few guys who've gone totally nuts for chicks they thought were crazy." Crazy chicks were the worst.

Or the best, depending on how you looked at it.

"He doesn't want me, Kai, I promise." The way she said it, like it hurt, needled me. She was mine and she shouldn't care about him anymore.

"You sound like you still want him." I sat up, the sheet pooling in my lap.

She rolled her eyes. "Please, not this again. Have I not made it clear how I feel about you? I don't want a house, or a baby, or someone else's baby for that matter, and yet I'm still here, unable to walk away."

We sat, separated, in a rickety moment of silence.

It was when I turned my head completely away from her that she sat up to wrap her legs around my waist and her arms around my torso.

"Kai, if I thought I could walk away from all that, if I thought I could walk away from you, I would. But I can't. You're the only thing holding me here."

She kissed my shoulder, and I pulled the sheet up around her, in case anyone was out there, watching.

"There's a gun," I told her, looking over to the nightstand, "and I think you should know it's here. I got it from my dad. It's in your drawer."

Her mouth froze against my skin. "There's a what?"

"I don't plan on using it, and I don't want you to, either." I reached for her chin to pull her face up where I could see it. "But in case we need it, it's here."

She pressed her lips into a tight line, which was a feat for them, and I wanted to cry at her beauty. She had reached inside me too, and I was a wholly different man than I'd been before, like she was the cocoon I'd needed to wrap myself up in for transformation. I was finally the type of person I'd previously looked at with a jealous disdain for having the wherewithal and determination to forge themselves into respectable and trustworthy individuals.

With grateful desperation, I worked her mouth with mine until that tight line loosened and she fell into me wholeheartedly. Then I made it up to her, for my previous lack of focus.

And she was right. It felt damn good to forget your troubles when you could.

24

PROOF IN HARD COPY

Kai

I shifted out from beneath her in the morning for the bathroom, and on my way back noticed the paper on the floor. Inside the bedroom door.

Under normal circumstances, I might have ignored it, but under these I stopped dead. What it looked like, if you were a suspicious sort, was that someone had slipped it under the door in the middle of the night.

How the hell could I have missed that?

The weather, that's how. It had been beating its way about the house for the last ten hours.

I wanted to cry as I dropped to my knees. Hell, I did a little, out of frustration. The folded paper sat there, taunting me. This had been my chance to kill the motherfucker, and I missed it.

Faryn's face appeared over the side of the bed. "What are you doing down there?"

I didn't answer.

"Are you crying?" Sitting up, she swung her legs around. At some point during the night, she'd pulled on her underwear and shirt. I looked down, feeling exposed, but it wasn't boxers I wanted. It was revenge.

"What's the matter?" She prodded me with her toe.

"He was here," I said, opening my fist to the note I'd crumpled in my grip.

"What do you mean, he was here?" But she didn't sound alarmed exactly. Wary. Wary was what she sounded.

I eyed her. She generally grabbed her clothes off the floor and pulled them back on under the covers, when she woke cold. But what if she'd been up, what if she'd let him in?

Of course, had I not done something like this before, maybe I wouldn't be so suspicious about someone doing it to me now. Karma was a bitch.

"Kai." That was better. A little more insistent, a little more panicked.

I unclenched my hand, smoothed the paper, and braced myself.

I'm disappointed you let Kai run around on a wild goose chase. It's insulting. It's also pointless to pretend I'm not in charge, and pointless for you to carry on like this with him. I'm not a patient sort of soul, and I won't wait forever. You know where this is headed, and there's nothing you can do to stop it. Kai won't stop it. Nothing will stop it. I will get what I want.

—L

"You do know," I stated levelly, though the rage was spreading from my now shaking hand. Clenching the paper, I told myself I needed to keep a clear head.

Was the innocent act all for my sake, to throw me off the scent? Could I really trust her? *Was* she carrying on with someone else?

Then again, that would be a good tactic for a psychotic asshole to take, in order to split us up. I rubbed my face with my hands and forced the question back in, the question of whether or not she was a liar.

When I had myself contained—for the time being—I was once again seeing clearly enough to notice the terror in her eyes. It went deeper than my anger took me, dense and deeply tethered, and dissolved any irritation I had for what she might be holding out on, any doubt for who she was. Releasing the note to the floor, I crawled up next to her and wrapped her tight in my arms.

She was cold, dead cold, and shaking.

"I need you to start over, from the beginning," I whispered. "Tell me about when it happened before, everything that's been going on now, and whoever you think this could be. Tell me every little piece of nothing that might mean something."

She swallowed tears, fighting for composure, and her words came out jagged. "I don't know. I honestly don't. I don't know anything anymore."

"Do you think someone might have followed you here?" But really, a stranger would easily be spotted. Word would've spread twelve minutes after they stepped across town lines.

"I didn't have a plan when I left and pretty much drove in random circles until I stopped. If someone had been following me, I would have lost them on the way." She buried her now wet cheeks against my bare chest. "And I didn't make the decision to leave until an hour before I left. No one could have known I was even going anywhere."

"Did you leave because you were scared?"

"I told you why I left."

I searched my brain for what she'd said that day in my unfinished kitchen. "So it had nothing to do with the stalker?"

She shook her head. "That was before, and it should've been over."

"Tell me about it."

"There's nothing to tell. The police found nothing." She straightened up to grab a tissue and blow her nose. "They turned my life upside down and found nothing." This brought on more emotion. "Then it stopped."

I looked at the letter. "Who did you think it was?"

She shook her head.

"Then why does this L person think you should know who he is?"

Her mouth dropped open a little, like it was an accusation. I tugged her back into me. "I'm sorry, I didn't mean it like that."

"Of course he thinks I should know who he is. He's an obsessed maniac, right?" Her eyes were desperate, pleading. Pleading for what, I didn't know. Pleading for me to believe her?

I took a deep breath, frustrated beyond frustrated with losing ground every step of the way. Fucker was giving me an inferiority complex, sneaking around right under my damn nose. I'd thought I was smarter than this. Tougher than anybody. With a pit bull determination that had never before been questioned.

How was I not beating this guy?

"Maybe we should call the cops," I suggested. "I hate the cops, but maybe we should call the cops."

"Why do you hate the cops?" she asked.

"Because they hate me. For all the shit I did to them as kids and all the trouble I caused as an—well, as an older kid." I heaved a sigh. "I suppose they can't be all bad though. Most of them married nice girls. That should say something, right?"

"I don't want to call the cops," she said. "They were useless last time." Sniffling, she looked up at me. "Can't we try to figure it out ourselves, at least until the warning comes? Or just…just run away together?"

I had a house being built, a baby on the way, and a lucrative business to inherit. But the idea still appealed to me. I would do anything, if it meant she was safe, if it meant she was mine.

Something stirred inside me, at the thought of escaping together from under this strain. And if I had to, I could build a new house, make a new baby, and start a new business.

I was a man now, and a man could do anything.

25

SECURITY

Faryn

October turned quite desolate. Or maybe that was simply how I perceived it, as that letter had colored life bleak.

Every day was a struggle, trying to keep it together, and the worry over losing my mind from the fear was perhaps greater than the fear itself. So I kept both locked up tight, sealed in oblivion, where Kai couldn't see the damage that was being done. This was saying something, what with his constant vigil.

He had proven himself again and again, somehow managing to stay levelheaded and sturdy while I stood next to him, bowed over by the storm. Pieces of me, on the other hand, were being worn away, cracking and falling off to be lost in the blustery winds.

The fact that his fancy motion detector had finally come in the mail and he was installing it didn't make me feel better. It made Kai feel better, though, as had the new doorknob and security chain. And the better he felt, the easier I found it to lie to myself.

I sat on the floor with my coffee, in what I suppose you could call the front hall, to watch him work.

"What about Minnesota?" I asked. "I've always wondered what it would be like to be penned in by months of heavy snow."

"Minnesota is too cold. What about Wyoming?"

"What's in Wyoming?"

"I don't know. What's in Minnesota?"

"Snow?"

He glanced back, and his grin made me curl. He made me curl. Dreaming of where we might run off to made me curl.

Feeling like ribbon rubbed raw by a pair of scissors, I rested my head against the wall and thought about this some more. We were stuck in a warm, cozy cabin—no, everyone dreamt of that. Okay, an old school house we'd bought and remodeled. It was the heart of winter, with knee deep snow out the front door and drifts that reached the windows. A cozy fire—that was necessary, even if overdone—and I had picked up an old guitar at an antique store—surely the nearest town to us in Minnesota, many, many miles away, would have an antique store. Kai was teaching me to play. Not sure he even knew how to play, but he was teaching me. I was in his lap, his arms molding mine to the instrument, when he interrupted us.

"Why wouldn't we head south?" he asked. "Florida, Texas, Louisiana, New Mexico."

I sighed as the snowflake burst. But I was adaptable. Or I would be, if it meant that much to him. "Georgia," I agreed. "We could buy a peach farm."

"I think they're called groves when they involve fruit trees."

"I like farms," I decided, sipping my coffee.

"Then a peach farm it is."

"On the other hand, I've always wondered what it might be like to own a restaurant. Not a diner or anything, but a small, quaint restaurant. Cute, charming, lovely ambience."

"I can only make burgers."

"And macaroni and cheese," I pointed out.

"Yes, and most people wouldn't want to come to a restaurant for boxed macaroni and cheese."

I grinned. "You could run the front of the house, and I could run the kitchen."

"You would be a stronger pull on customers. Nobody would come for me."

"Oh, you were thinking strip joint?" I asked.

He gave me a look, and I set my coffee down as if he'd dared me. I stood and moved to the slow, languid music pulsing softly out of his phone. Having no practice at this sort of thing, I could only hope that as I finished my turn, he wouldn't be snickering. For incentive, I began to tease my sweater up, only to find Savannah standing behind him in the hall.

I dropped my sweater as our eyes locked, and she whistled. Kai's head spun around and he tried to close the door on her.

Stopping it with her foot, she shoved it back open.

I sank back to my spot on the floor. "Hi, Savannah."

"Hi, sugar. Hi, baby daddy."

Kai and I shared a look. We'd decided she was lying about the whole pregnancy thing. This, at least, made it easier to play along. She was supposedly four months now, and though wearing large, flowing, mommy-to-be tops, she was still slight as ever.

"I thought you'd both be working today," she said. "And by that, I mean I stopped by the store *and* Chuck's, before making my way over here. Needless to say, I could use some refreshment." Stepping by Kai, she made her way to my sink and turned the tap on, drinking right from it.

"Which was fine," she continued with a wet chin, once finished. "Because that means I got to tell everybody about our baby's uterus." This was her newest hobby, bothering us at work about the development going on inside her body, as if the three of us were building a city. "She's almost half a foot long. Half a foot! And has this furry hair stuff all over her body." She made a face. "Well, I'm sure she's cute anyway. Most important, she has a uterus!"

"Great," Kai muttered.

"It's important," she scolded him. "A uterus is very important."

"If it's a girl, it's important," I agreed.

She grinned at me before sidestepping to help herself to a

cup of coffee.

"That's not good for the baby," I said.

"I have two things to say to that," she replied. "One, if I can't have alcohol, I'm having coffee. And two, the internet said she should be kicking soon, and if coffee doesn't make her kick, I don't know what will."

She patted her stomach and sat next to me.

"Are you planning on staying a while?" I wondered. This was my place, after all. Chuck's was one thing, but my apartment?

She winked at me over her mug and took a sip. "Maybe, if things get exciting."

"Don't count on it," Kai mumbled.

Savannah rolled her eyes. "You've become such a wet blanket, Kai. I mean, who even are you anymore? I bet you're not even dressing up for Halloween this year."

He snorted. "I've never dressed up for Halloween."

She straightened her shoulders, clearly offended. "Well, poo-pooey on you. I have big plans for us."

"Like what?" he asked.

"Like trick or treating, of course." She patted her belly. "Baby's first Halloween. Plus, everyone knows Halloween costumes are the next best thing to stripper costumes, and then I can see Faryn all dolled up like she is in my dreams."

I made a face.

"Oh, come on." She elbowed me. "Loosen up a little. How much fun would a Halloween party be? You could totally sell that to Chuck, to have everyone in the bar in costume. It would be rad. Let's see." She tapped her skinny pink lips with a fingertip. "What's a famous foursome we could go as?"

"Savannah, are you mad?" Kai swung his head to us. "You can't dress the baby until it comes out of you. And no one is going to give you candy for a fetus."

"I'm not talking about the baby, lover. I'm talking about Andy." She carefully pasted a beaming grin on her face. "You, me, Faryn, and Andy."

I bit my lip. Kai had pronounced Andy good as dead.

To be expected, Kai tossed the drill down on the floor and stood. He slammed the door shut, turned the motion detector on, opened the door, nodded as the alarm went off, and stalked off to the living room.

I collected my tools, carefully replacing them in my small box, then slid them back in the front hall closet.

With a huff, Savannah stood and followed Kai. I was close behind.

"You know," she started, "it's not very nice how you ignore him whenever he tries to talk to you. You haven't even let him apologize."

"I don't know what you're talking about." He stood at the windows, looking out over Chuck's to the homes beyond, his jaw tight and his words tighter.

"Are you kidding me? He has tried a million different ways to get you to listen to him. You don't think, after a lifetime of friendship, you can at least give him a minute?"

He spun around, eyes dangerous. "Give who a minute? I do not know who you are talking about."

"Kai, please."

"No, Savannah, and you have now officially overstayed

your nonexistent welcome. Go. And do not make me ask you again."

She shifted from foot to foot as he glared at her.

"Fine." She shoved her mug at my chest. "I'll go. But I'm not going away, and I'm not giving up. On you, *or* you and Andy." She spoke to him this time, as if I had fallen by the wayside. Ultimately, her talk of me being part of the family was just that—talk—and what she truly wanted was me out of the picture.

After she stormed out, I walked to the kitchen and set her cup in the sink. The true blue ceramic clashed with the ancient olive green basin, and I was struck with the realization that it was, indeed, me who didn't fit. If it weren't for me, her life would have turned out just the way she'd envisioned it.

I couldn't help but think I'd had this same effect on Lia.

WINTER

26

CLOSING IN

Faryn

I'm not a patient sort of soul, and I won't wait forever . . .

I closed my eyes and braced my hands on the kitchen counter, but two months later, these words were still etched in my brain, rather than on the tile countertop where they might disappear.

They never disappeared. And they never stopped taunting.

Reaching up into the cupboard for a coffee filter, I felt Kai's hands at my waist, sliding their way under my shirt to rest on my tummy. He kissed the back of my neck, and I relaxed back into him.

His smell was enchanting, always, but especially coming off a shower. Twisting to face him, I let my fingers fall across his bare chest, content that in moments like these, at least, I was charmed forgetful.

"Let me take you to brunch," he whispered, lips lightly on mine.

"You can take me wherever you want," I told him.

"I want to take you to brunch." He grinned slightly and pulled away, heading toward the bedroom in a towel.

"Do we have time for a detour?"

"You mean, to a land far, far away?" he asked, disappearing into the closet.

It was a pleasant fantasy—escape—but in reality, I'd tried that once. It hadn't been the magic cure-all I'd hoped for, so I had to assume a second relocation would be no different.

More thoughts, again marching up to taunt me. In a swift defensive move, I stood on the edge of the bed and unbuttoned my jeans. When Kai emerged to see this, he was in the midst of pulling on a shirt. One look and he yanked it back off.

Resting his face on my belly, he wrapped his arms up around me, and I melted fully into him. The thing I liked best about winter was the body heat. Particularly another person's and how you could warm yourself with it.

The aftereffects of being with Kai, same as the ones from sitting in front of a hot fire for too long, were reluctant to wear off, and I felt the fading embers on my skin as we drove to the diner and settled in a booth.

"What are you smiling about?" he asked, sitting down across from me. Except he knew. He was smirking.

At least there was that, at least there was us. Our

relationship was only getting better, richer, more intricately detailed. I grinned wider and turned the question on him. "What are *you* smiling about?"

He chuckled, and I let myself get caught in it, wishing it could bind me up tighter until there was no room left for my fears. I slid my foot out of my boot and up between his legs in order to pull another. It worked.

The door chimed, and what he could see over my shoulder turned his face with just a glance. Only three people could do that, none of whom had a place in the moment we'd been having.

Twisting in my seat, I found Savannah on target to join us, Andy trailing behind her.

This whole time, I'd assumed we'd leave for my sake, but suddenly it occurred to me it might be useful for Kai, too. Everyone close to him had let him down, and everyone he'd at one point thought he'd had, he no longer wanted. Perhaps he would appreciate not being faced with them every day, perhaps he itched to run as much as I did, and perhaps it wasn't such a futile idea after all.

Savannah slid in next to me and wafted my scent toward her, breathing it up as if I were a bed of roses.

Only then did she ask, "Mind if we join you?"

"Yes," Kai grumbled.

"Oh don't be like that," she said. "Just because I'm hot for your girlfriend—and want you to marry me—doesn't mean we can't have brunch together."

"I think it does," he responded.

Andy had not yet sat down, and his presence was imposing

like an elephant in the room. Savannah and I both stared at him.

"Kai," he finally said. It was a defeated plea, as Kai still refused to acknowledge his existence.

"Andy," Kai clipped in response, a huge step forward, though he wouldn't look at him.

"Haven't we been friends too long to end it like this?"

"Maybe you should've asked yourself that before you attacked my girlfriend." Kai's eyes were on me, empty, hollow, which was also an improvement over the previous crushing rage. I gave him a sympathetic look, uncomfortable being the roadblock between them, even if Andy did spread across my senses like poison ivy.

"Oh, get over it," Savannah snapped. "With those lips, Faryn may as well walk around with a sign on her head—*for a good time, kiss here*."

I pulled them into my mouth.

"Still luscious," she informed, rolling her eyes to Andy. "Sit, would you? You're making me nervous."

He did, on the edge of Kai's seat with a mumble.

"Louder," Savannah told him. "Use your balls, Andy, and speak up."

"I'm sorry, Faryn," he said.

I raised an eyebrow, and Kai looked over to him for the first time.

"I'm sorry," he repeated. "You're a very good-looking woman, but it wasn't okay for me to lose control of myself like I did."

Savannah's lips moved along with his, as if she'd scripted

it, but I wasn't going to point that out to Kai. The way I figured, the fewer conflicts in my life the better.

"I was confused and upset and I'm not very good at controlling my actions under those circumstances. It won't happen again."

Savannah grinned and nodded, looking around the table for our reaction.

Kai stared at him, incredulous.

"Thank you, Andy," I said. "I appreciate the apology."

"Can we pretend it never happened?" he asked.

"Of course, I think that's a fine idea," I responded.

"I agree," Savannah said. "Kai, don't you think that's a fine idea?"

Kai looked at me. I gave him a sad smile. He looked at Savannah, who gave him a jubilant one.

"Actually, I think it's a terrible idea," he finally said.

"Please, bro," Andy pleaded. "Hear me out."

"I don't need to hear anything out. Nothing will make it okay."

"It's not like we haven't done shit like that before."

"When the girl was willing, Andy," Kai seethed. "When the girl was fucking willing."

"Why's it matter?" Savannah asked. "You've never done something stupid you've regretted?"

The silence at the table threatened to turn toxic. I worked my toes a bit to lessen the sting. Kai frowned though, and this time blocked himself from my foot.

He eventually flipped open a menu, and the rest of us followed. Andy awkwardly waited for Kai to hand one down but he didn't, so I passed two to Savannah.

The waitress soon came for our order, which broke the dark silence for light conversation. This continued after she left, and though we needed a few jump-starts, the further into it we got, the more relaxed it became. Kai was careful not to speak directly to Andy, but they were both in the conversation, which again, was something. Savannah rattled on about the baby, Kai pulled my foot back closer to him, Andy asked about the house, which almost derailed things, and I told them stories from work.

Savannah helped herself to everyone's plate, and aside from trying to feed me a few forkfuls of her own, the meal ended as pleasantly as it could have.

"We should do this more often," Savannah said as the waitress cleared our table.

Kai and I shared a look, but Andy agreed.

"Hey, wanna see my belly?" Savannah asked. "I'm finally starting to pop."

And before I could tell her I didn't, she lifted up her shirt until I was not only facing my denial in the face, but also the bottom half of her lacy teal bra.

She saw my eyes there, an easier sight for me than the baby bump, and blew a kiss in my general direction.

My hope crumbled around me once again, and I tried to pull my foot from Kai's lap. He held onto it. His gaze was steady in mine, as if this didn't matter, as if it didn't change anything.

But all the happily-ever-after scenarios I'd played out in my head the last few months, scenarios I hadn't realized I'd come to depend on for my faltering sanity, were now flashing amended before my eyes, with Savannah and Kai's baby inside them.

It was crowded.

I pushed at her to get out of the booth, and she complied. She walked to the door with me, and we stood outside until Kai and Andy had paid and joined us.

"It's been kicking, too," Andy said, putting a hand on Savannah's stomach. "Wanna feel?"

Kai and I shook our heads, like they were attached to the same string and manned by the same hand, and without discussion, we turned to walk away.

"Hey!" Savannah cried. "Daddy doesn't get to leave without a hug." And she pressed her now rounded tummy up against the body that had been all over me hours before.

I almost vomited into the black slush in the parking lot while Kai extricated himself, then sat stone-faced in the Jeep as he drove me to work.

Pulling to a stop in Chuck's lot, he asked if I was okay.

I shook my head. "I don't think I am."

"Because of Savannah?"

"I think I was really counting on the fact that she was lying." I said this to my hands, to myself.

He sighed out a shaky breath. "Yeah. Me, too."

"But she's not."

"Nope, she sure isn't."

I looked up at him. "I think I'm in shock."

He nodded. "I'm pretty disappointed, too."

"We aren't taking off, are we?" I asked. "We aren't going

to leave all this behind."

"I didn't get the impression you really wanted to."

I leaned into him, a request for his arms around me, and he obliged. We sat in silence for ten minutes, our future morphing as our dreams ran away, and then I had to get back to my life.

"Want me to come in with you?" he asked.

"I thought you were going to work for a few hours."

"I was going to," he said. "But if you need me…"

"You can't save me from myself, Kai. I wish you could, but it's unrealistic." This was the healthy way to look at it. We forgot that sometimes, let ourselves toe the line of dependence, and it would do me good to remember I was in charge of myself, and only I could fix me. "You're just a guy."

"Just a guy," he repeated with a grimace. "Ouch."

I looked at him, at the wound my words had opened on his face. "Just *the* guy," I amended. "The only guy I've ever come across who makes me feel whole, and the only one I'll ever feel this way about. Just *that* guy."

He fingered my hair, and I lost myself in his dark eyes. "Okay, I can live with being that guy," he finally said.

Wanting more, I prompted him, "Tell me I'm not just a girl."

"I was not the one who used that phrase. And I wouldn't have said you couldn't save me because you have saved me. I couldn't have dreamt you up, even in my wildest fantasies."

I nibbled on his ear. "Think we could play out some of those wild fantasies later tonight?"

Catching my lips on his, he mumbled, "They've all been

played out. I'm living them."

Our body heat swirled the car foggy until I rested my forehead on his cheek. But I had to go. And as I made my way across that parking lot, it felt as if I was walking away from him forever.

I could only hope that wasn't the case. But as I stood behind the bar, my hope drained out slowly while the hours ticked by. Taking its place was a restless desperation and visions of Savannah's belly, growing until it exploded. And though I tried to slow my thoughts down, one would force its way through from my subconscious with each Dark and Stormy I mixed for Lewis.

Why had I come here?

I'd been searching for a place where an entrancing calm might find me, for a life synonymous with simplicity and solitude. All so I could center myself and figure out who I was, instead of who circumstances had forced me to be. I'd wanted to pull myself together, into one cohesive unit that did not contradict itself.

Was I whole? Or was I still fractured and restless?

Kai kept me anchored and soothed, but that couldn't last forever, not in the face of babies and houses. It hadn't lasted with Spencer, but Kai was nothing if not resilient. Spencer didn't have his kind of fortitude.

Had I managed to forget the pain?

For the most part. But looking a four-year-old in the face—a six, seven, eight-year-old—remembering not only those years of mine, but also those of my siblings, when I'd taken over for my parents, that wouldn't help me leave those tormented feelings of loss behind.

Was my life simpler and less complicated?

Perhaps, but it was still overwhelmingly messy. Savannah had made sure of that. The letters had made sure of that.

Had I found solitude?

Absolutely not. Between Leon and Philip at home, and Chuck and Lewis here, solitude was a fleeting, distant memory. The city had held more isolation, as one in a million, than the peace and quiet of the country did.

And most importantly, had I figured out who I was and what I wanted?

I wanted Kai, that was the only conclusion I'd come to. His presence had sidetracked me from focusing on anything else. So what did that mean? That I should lose him for the sake of doing what I'd set out to do?

Or didn't it really matter who I was meant to be? Perhaps it was pointless to define such a thing before becoming it. Perhaps what mattered was who I loved and how I chose to spend my time. Perhaps I should stop searching and start living.

At least I didn't feel pulled in a million directions anymore, now that there was only Kai to take from me and not the demands of business and family. But that splintered feeling still wouldn't go away—like I was someone, but maybe also someone else.

I shook my head, realizing that with each of these questions came a subtle helping of anxiety, and now as they all spun on the surface, they joined forces and hit me with an overwhelming sense of failure.

In the face of that, I ran to the bathroom and spent half an hour vomiting into the toilet. Needless to say, Chuck could hear it from the hall and made me go home early.

As I walked across the street, the stark emptiness of the trees mocked me. It was hard to believe they'd once held so much promise, back when I'd taken their new spring growth as a sign of what this chapter of my life might bring.

You couldn't run from your problems, of course I'd heard that. They did, after all, so often come from within. And perhaps it had been silly of me to hold out hope, but it was the one thing I'd had.

Well, no longer.

With a sigh and the crunch of gravel beneath my feet, I released the last shred of it, indeed feeling quite empty as it loosened its fingers and blew away.

Unlocking the door, I made my way to the couch. My gaze settled absently out the windows at the gray marbled sky, and I resisted the urge to call Kai. He was probably finishing up at work and would come right away, but it was only just getting dark, and I needed to sort through a few things.

If I chose Kai and his baby, then responsibility would swoop back in to clutch me in its pointy beak. But if I chose myself, and the path I'd been aiming for when I came here—if I walked away from him—I would break my own heart, surely splintering myself completely in two.

27

FREEDOM

Kai

All day I'd thought about what Savannah had said at the diner, how Andy had been my family when no one else bothered, and how without him, I wouldn't have made it through some of the shit I'd started.

I'd thought about it until I was sick of thinking about it. So after work, while Faryn was still safe and sound at Chuck's, I spread out on the couch in my apartment to give my mind a break. After about an hour staring at the ceiling, I fell asleep, only to wake from a knock at the door.

Groggy and disoriented, I checked my watch. It was almost bar time, but I had a minute. I ran my hands across my face, trying to wake myself up, and by the time I rolled off the couch, Andy had begun to pound and call my name.

"Yeah, yeah," I yelled. "I'm coming."

Unlocking the door while shutting the alarm off on my phone, I stepped aside to let him in. He looked around like I might actually ask him to stay awhile.

"I'm supposed to meet Faryn at Chuck's in twenty minutes," I told him, trying to keep it at the door and keep it quick.

"Oh, right."

It was Saturday, so really she'd probably be cleaning up 'til half past two. This gave me enough time to accept the apology and have a drink with an old friend, if I wanted to. But did I want to?

Was I a girl now? Because toiling over this all day had sure made me feel like one.

Taking a few steps into the kitchen, I waved him in and headed for the fridge. "Wanna beer?" I asked.

He gave me a toothy grin and sat on a stool. Tapping cans, we took long first drinks.

"It's been a while since we've done this," I realized.

"I'll apologize again, if you want me to," he said. "Whatever it takes to put this Faryn thing behind us."

Son of a bitch would be smarter to keep his mouth shut. If he wanted me to forget about it, he should stop bringing it up.

"Is it behind us?" he asked.

I clenched and unclenched my jaw, not wanting to make an actual decision on the matter. "Why don't we just have our beer and see how it goes?"

But then he had to go and make it worse. "Faryn okay this morning?"

"Huh?" Did I really need to clarify that he should never speak of her again?

"She seemed off this morning when you guys left."

I raised an eyebrow. "You know her real well, Andy, to know if she was on or off?"

"Aw, come on Kai. Don't start that again. I'm just sayin'. You eat dinner with someone and they actin' weird, a person feels that."

I crossed my arms. "You've had dinner with her?"

He rolled his eyes. "Breakfast, sorry. My bad."

I eyed him, but he held strong.

"Let's start over," he suggested.

Fine. I shook my head of it and asked the standard opening question. "So how you been?"

"Fantastic, actually. You?"

I shrugged. I was a whole lot of contradicting things right now that I could hardly sort out. "Why so fantastic?" It was not a word generally found in his vocabulary.

"Well, I don't know. All around, things couldn't be much better."

"Yeah?" I furrowed my brow at him and thought about this a second. Usually, the only thing going well for him was his job. What else was there?

"Yeah." He grinned wide into his beer, and I couldn't help but see it—he'd had sex, and it had been recently. Come to think of it, why would he have been with Savannah this morning, if it were another girl that was going well for him?

"You and Savannah today," I started. "You two gettin' together?"

"Nah, she just wants advice. You know, on how to get you back and all."

But he wasn't looking at me anymore. I'd known Andy a long time, and I knew Andy couldn't lie for shit. That was why I'd always done the lying for the both of us. "What'd you tell her?" I asked.

"To hang in there."

"And why the hell would you tell her something like that?"

"'Cuz it's your baby, Kai." He spoke it like this should make all the difference, like he knew how it felt to truly be attached to another living thing, connected intrinsically like I felt with Faryn. This made me more suspicious.

"So what?" I countered. "A lot of parents aren't together. Ours ain't."

"You're building a house," he said. "And houses are for families." Interestingly enough, the bastard seemed irritated with me.

"Not for Savannah's family," I stated.

He sneered a little. I could tell he was trying to keep his disgust from showing, but he'd never been too good at that, either. "So you're just gonna leave her hanging?"

"I ever strike you as respectable before?"

"Well, no, but now you do." His eyes turned mean. "Or maybe that's only a show for Faryn."

I met those eyes with some of my own, daring him to get nasty with me. "It's not a show," I promised. "And I'll do right by that baby. But Faryn's moving into that house. Not

Savannah."

"Fuck, somebody gotta build her a house." He tried to wipe his expression clean with a few more swigs of beer, but it came out looking mildly tortured instead. "If you ain't gonna do it, then maybe I will."

"That supposed to make me want her or something?"

"No, she deserves a house. A steady home to raise that kid in, an environment that fosters love and learnin', not like the places we grew up." Said like he was attached to Savannah. Or maybe even the baby.

And it began to dawn on me. "But you don't want a house, Andy. You never have. And you never wanted a baby."

"Well, maybe I do now."

"Yeah, why's that?"

"Who cares why?"

"I do."

"What, you can change but no one else can? Maybe the rest of us are ready to grow up too. You ain't got no monopoly on it." He downed his beer and stood up, red in the face like I was mistreating someone he loved.

"It's yours," I said, astounded. Why hadn't I thought of this before? "It's fucking yours."

"What?"

"The baby." I laughed with the glee of a mystery solved. "It's yours!"

"Naw, it ain't mine," he stammered. Again, the guy couldn't lie for shit.

"Let's go on over and ask her then." Grabbing my jacket and keys, I headed for the front door, turning in the small front hall when I didn't hear him behind me. Looking back, I found him immobile in the same spot.

Oh yeah, and now he realized he was in trouble. Sure as shit, that baby was not mine.

Faryn would be fucking ecstatic to hear about this. As for me, I could hardly comprehend it, that in the blink of an eye with no work whatsoever, half our problems simply disappeared.

But I had to make sure, had to confront Savannah with Andy by my side.

"Come on," I commanded. "Now."

Like the henchman he used to be, his obedience kicked in, and he came. I drove the Jeep over the few blocks to Savannah's and got out. Andy didn't, but I knew he would eventually, so I made my way to her front steps alone and began ringing the bell nonstop.

She finally opened the door, hair all over the place and one of her lace nighties on. I had a hard time believing she slept in those every night, because they sure as shit didn't look comfortable, and I'd never dated anyone else who used them for anything but foreplay. This one parted down the middle, which meant it revealed her bare belly.

"Don't they make maternity lingerie?" I asked, recognizing it for one I'd seen before.

"Who needs maternity lingerie?" she responded. "I ain't ashamed of this."

I pushed in past her, listening to her greet Andy behind me. And all the proof I needed was right there: not in her words—a simple "hey, Andy"—but in the tone she used. It was a sugary voice she'd only ever used on me when we were fucking very, very regularly.

I headed for the kitchen and planted myself in the center of it. "That baby isn't mine, is it?"

They were both standing in the doorway, smushed next to each other like they'd gotten stuck on their way through.

"Of course it is," Savannah said, her hand finding her stomach.

"It ain't Andy's?"

"Why would it be Andy's?"

"I wouldn't put it past either of you to do this on purpose. Lie about a baby to get what you want. Kinda makes me wonder if it was an accident, or if you planned the baby before you even had it."

"You think we care that much?" Andy asked. "To lie about a baby?"

"I wouldn't sleep with anyone else, Kai," Savannah insisted. "You're the only man I love. You're the only man I've ever loved."

Andy choked a little and looked over to her. She scowled at him and moved forward, inching into my space, pleading with her eyes and breasts, which she'd shoved out in the lead, and which, I had to say, were looking much more rounded than the last time I'd seen them.

"Then fuck me now," I proposed, "right here in this kitchen. In front of him."

Like I was watching a movie that skipped, her movement hiccupped from one moment to the next, choppy because she knew she was caught and didn't know what to do about it.

265

"You mean a threesome?" she asked warily.

"No. He watches." Staring at her with loathing, for all the turmoil she'd caused us, I began to undo my pants.

She threw her shoulders back and began to lift her top off, but Andy stopped her. "No!" Rushing up, he pushed her arms down, wrapped himself around her, and covered her from my eyes.

She fought him off. "What are you doing?" she hissed.

"I don't want you to go back to him!" he cried. Pounding his fist against his chest, he continued, "*I* love you! *I* appreciate you! Not him! How can't you see that?"

"But, I thought that's what you wanted," she whispered. "This was your idea, remember?"

"Maybe it was, but now I want you. *And* my baby. I'll even build you a house."

They stared at each other a minute. Savannah looked back to me, confused.

"What does he have that I don't?" Andy asked her.

"Oh, Andy." She threw her arms around him. "He has nothing you don't, except a hot girlfriend that I'd love to get my hands on. And in two months that won't matter anymore."

"Aha!" I cried. She was lying about when she was due, too. And here I'd thought for a minute he was sleeping with her while I was. Sadly, that restored the bit of my ego I hadn't realized I'd lost.

But they weren't paying attention to me. And apparently Andy didn't care what I might see as long as it was his paws all over it instead of mine. Gingerly stepping around them so as not to touch any body parts, I ran my ass to the Jeep.

I had to get to Faryn. I had to tell her the good news.

28

SERENITY FOUND

Faryn

I woke up freezing and grabbed the blanket off the back of the couch to wrap myself up.

This absentmindedness flitted out the open windows however, as soon as I realized that they were indeed wide open. Most certainly not how I'd left them. Fear rose in my throat, and I patted the couch next to me where I'd left my phone. The spot was empty.

Scrambling, I tripped on the blanket and banged my knee against the coffee table, whimpering at the pain as I limped over to shove the panes down. They were old, with many layers of paint, and did not move easily. Whoever had done this, had they been trying to wake me? Had they been setting me up as an easy target, knowing I'd close them, and while doing so turn my back to the room?

I flung around with squinted eyes, afraid of what would greet me, what I might see.

All was still, in the living room anyway, and I sidestepped with back and palms against the far wall, making my way for the kitchen through that side, rather than the hall by the bathroom and front door. One could circle this main area of my apartment, living room to kitchen to front hall, past the bathroom and back into the living room, and the thought that someone might be just out of sight, no matter how well I checked, had my hands trembling as they felt their way. I shook from the inside, almost as if the panic and anxiety were splitting me open, cracking me up from the center.

Holding my breath as I came through the open doorway, I sobbed it out when I found the kitchen empty. Grabbing a knife off the block, I continued to the front hall where the door was unlocked.

I hadn't set the alarm, knowing Kai would be coming, but had I really left the door unlocked? And now what did I do? Did I lock it, assuming someone was out there and I'd be safe inside, or leave it open, assuming someone was waiting for me in here and I'd be fleeing through it shortly?

More than anything, I didn't want to be cornered, so with knife in hand, I left it open and flipped on the light in the bathroom. My hand was shaky and missed its mark twice, because I could not stop imagining how someone might jump out to grab me, or stab me, or who-knows-what me.

When light finally flooded the small space, I slipped the

rest of myself in, closing the door behind me so I could deal with the bathtub a little easier. I tried not to think of all the times I'd been on the other side of a shower curtain, terrified that when I reached for my towel it would be handed to me by an intruder.

I used to worry my little sister would find me naked and bloody in the tub.

My heart thumped an irregular beat in my ear, faltering with every move I made and unable to make it through without holding its own breath.

I pierced the shower curtain desperately and violently, but the knife hit nothing on the other side. Backing up, I bent forward at my waist and threw it open.

No one was there.

I crumpled to the floor in sobs, acutely aware there was one more room to go. And the closets. Oh God, the closets.

Kai. I drew my strength from Kai. I thought of him, and it bolstered me to stand, albeit with the help of the wall, and I readjusted my hold on the knife.

Why hadn't I gone for the gun in my bedroom? I didn't want to get near enough a crazy person to knife them, if that's what it came to.

I swung out to the linen closet in the hall. Shelving, it was shelving in there so maybe I didn't need to be scared of that. With an eye on the bedroom, I quietly slid open the bi-fold door.

No one was curled up and stuffed among my towels, but it occurred to me that while I'd been closed up in the bathroom, someone would've had ample time to sneak around the rest of the apartment. Would they be waiting for me in the living room as I passed, or were they following me from the kitchen behind? Biting down on my lip so hard it bled, I shot across the worn, slippery wood into my room, fumbled for the gun in my drawer, threw it out in front of me, and swung it around.

I felt like a crazy person.

It wasn't the first time.

But who wouldn't be crazy right now?

Where had my phone gone? Why couldn't I find my phone? And where was Kai?

I dropped to my belly and pointed the gun under the bed frame, lifted up the bed skirt, didn't find anyone.

Crawling across the floor, I looked under the closet door. My shoes were lined up neatly, but anyone could be standing among them. I'd never know.

Lifting myself up to all fours, I gripped the gun as tightly as I could. Then up on my knees. One foot flat, then up to two.

I was not sure I'd be able to overcome the fear and open the closet door. And then, after trying, I was sure. Sure that I would not be able to overcome the fear.

Closing my eyes, I shot into it instead. Four times.

No screams, no nothing, but for the reverb of the gun in my ears, in my head.

Well, maybe the gunshot would bring someone—Kai, the police, Leon, anyone.

Back to the living room where I nearly slipped on a piece of paper. Had that been there when I woke? Or had it been dropped while I searched the apartment?

Scanning the place one more time from where I stood, I dropped to my knees to retrieve it, then slid against the wall, beneath the windows for safety, for sight of anything that might be coming at me, in order to read it.

I can't do this any longer. Probably pointless even, to write you, since you know what's coming, what I want, what I've been after for a long time now. But I needed to apologize. I am sorry I have to take you down with me, truly. You've put up a good fight, and no one can say you didn't try—thank you for that—but I was right: nothing will ever fix us. Nothing can take the torment away.

—L

Kai had been wrong; he couldn't protect me.

I'd hoped he was right, had forced myself to believe it was someone in town, but it didn't matter, my denial was pointless. I would never get away from her. I could move from town to town and life to life, but she would always be there.

I let the gun fall out of my grip, ready now to face the fight that had been a long time coming, and ripped her letter to shreds. Opening the window above me an inch, I let each sliver dangle out into the night before letting it go on the wind.

29

GOODBYES
Faryn

The next thing I registered was Kai's face, angelic and leaning over mine. I tried to reach for it, to feel his cheek under my fingertips, but my body wasn't cooperating.

"They're coming, Faryn, the ambulance is coming." He was whispering, but I could hear him so clearly. Beautiful juicy drops of tears were falling directly on me—so pretty in slow motion. "Stay with me," he gasped. "Please God stay with me."

"I love you, Kai," I managed to squeeze out. It was imperative he know. "I love you and you've meant everything to me."

"Don't say that! Don't talk like that! You're fine! You'll be fine!" Yet he was staring at my gut in horror. I'd put up a good fight. A gunshot to the abdomen, well, it could have been worse. But timing hadn't been on my side.

I could tell I was bleeding out, if that was even possible. It was as if in this place, half here and half there, I simply knew everything. Every cell of my body was aware and communicating with my brain, to an extent it never had the capability of doing before.

Granted, it was awfully painful, but if I concentrated on the low hum above the physical agony, it morphed numb and I could close my eyes and easily imagine the gunshot wound to my stomach, as good as if I'd seen it myself.

"Don't close your eyes! Don't leave me!" His voice had never been so desperate, as if he were hanging onto the same thread that I was.

I forced them open, but they fluttered in my weakness.

"Please, you can't leave me." His head dropped to my chest, and his rocking sobs hurt, but I couldn't tell him. I couldn't say it. I wanted him close, more than I wanted the pain to go away.

"At least you have the baby," I managed out. At least I wasn't leaving him with nothing.

"It's not mine," he cried. "It's not mine. It's Andy's. It's always been Andy's. And I..." He choked on his anguish. "All I want is you."

"I'm so sorry, Kai." My mouth was full of liquid, or it felt that way. Like I had a sore throat and was trying to gargle salt water. I remembered when my mom used to make me do that as a kid. And I remembered when Lia used to make me do it, for an altogether different reason.

He dropped his head, and his wail filled the room.

"I'm so sorry I couldn't keep her off," I told him. "I'm so sorry I failed you."

"What are you talking about? You can't give up, don't give up!" His head whipped back, and I heard noise, but sounds of any sort were no longer clear. Sadly, even Kai was no longer clear.

"Lia." I spewed it out with everything I had in me, before it was too late. "It was Lia."

And then the blackness swept in.

30

INNOCENCE IN TRUTH

Kai

It took them four days to release me.

Not like I could blame them for the arrest. My fingerprints were the only ones in the apartment, aside from Faryn's, and the blood had been dripping off me by the time the paramedics arrived.

I knew I shouldn't have touched her, knew that doing so might cause problems with evidence, but she'd been white as a sheet, otherworldly, and I couldn't stop myself from clinging onto her, from trying to keep her.

It had been my gun that I'd brought into her house, and for that guilt alone I felt jail was where I belonged.

At first, I wasn't a suspect. Until there was no one else and

I was. Until my cries about the letter bottomed out in the absence of proof—I couldn't find the one we'd read that morning, and I'd searched so hard I tore up the place. That probably hadn't looked very good, either.

They'd believed me for a while, but I'd been who I'd been, and they couldn't look past that.

The funeral had been small. Me, Chuck, Leon, Lewis, Philip, Savannah, Andy, and a handful of others who frequented the bar. Otherwise, Faryn kept to herself, and I'd had no luck tracing her family.

A few days later, they'd arrested me. I'd gone willingly and now I was walking out.

They hadn't told me why, but I wasn't going to complain. I couldn't lay myself over her grave like I wanted to, while still locked up.

I followed blindly to the holding area where they released my things and deposited them numbly onto my person: wallet, keys, Faryn's key. I held onto it tightly, wishing I had something more of hers, something I could wear, something I could keep, something that might help me feel like she wasn't gone.

I didn't know how I was going to get through this without her, how I'd get through losing her, if she weren't here to hand me over the strength.

Taking a few tentative steps, I lifted my head to a group of five. They looked oddly familiar. Well, all but one.

"Kai Allen?" this one asked.

"Yes?"

He took a step forward and reached out his hand. "Spencer

Larson. I'm so sorry you had to go through this."

The fiancé. I nearly stumbled.

A sandy-haired man stepped up next to him. "I'm Finn. I understand you and Lia were close."

I blinked. "I'm sorry?"

"You and Lia? They said you were serious."

I looked at the others, the small girl with short layered hair, and the two boys who had the same secretive look in their eyes I'd had at that age, in my early twenties.

"Faryn," I said. "Faryn and I were serious." I almost told them Lia was the one who'd killed her, but I was tired of trumpeting that story. And even I didn't know what to believe anymore.

It didn't matter. They exchanged glances anyway, like the police had begun to do a few short days before they arrested me.

Spencer breathed out a sigh, then stepped up to pull me aside, over by the chairs that ran along the wall. I went willingly. Without Faryn, I was so destitute it didn't matter what anyone did to me. I had no fight left.

"I don't know how to say this," he started, wringing his hands together. "So I'm just gonna say it. Faryn was Lia's alter."

"Excuse me?"

"I was in love with Lia. I knew she had dissociative identity disorder, but I thought she had it all worked out. You know, had brought them back together or whatever. Faryn had been her first, and strongest, and I guess... Well, things were going fine I thought, and then four weeks before our wedding, she up and disappeared."

I dropped down into the seat behind me, buried my head in my hands, and tried to grasp what he was saying.

Many minutes later, he sat next to me, and the movement pulled me from a void.

"You didn't know?" he asked.

I shook my head, unable to speak.

"You want to?"

I didn't respond. I didn't know that, either.

Just as I was about to slip back into the sweetness of a black hole, he cleared his throat. "They say a personality can only split when you're real young. Lia's father wasn't *their* father," Spencer looked over to the others. "And he, well, he did stuff to her. A lot of stuff. Stuff you couldn't even begin to imagine. When her mom found out, she left him, ran away, disappeared. It was the only way, really. She promised Lia she'd start a new life for them, start over, promised this was better than getting revenge, than making him pay. She met Frank almost right away and they started a new life.

"Lia had a lot of anger issues—anxiety, depression—but she was magical and enchanting too. Anyway, Faryn was levelheaded, softer, oblivious sort of. The therapist referred to Faryn as a helper, rather than, you know, sometimes you see the angry protector. Lia said she had enough anger for both of them, and Faryn used to talk her down, comfort her. Faryn kept Lia from hurting herself, lashing out, acting out, hunting down her father, things like that. I'm not sure I would've known, if she hadn't told me, but once I did know, I noticed a few things, here and there. It wasn't much, wasn't a big deal, wasn't enough to keep me from loving her. The stress of the wedding, though…"

The void danced at my periphery, blissfully promising to take me away, but Spencer's face twisted, and he looked away to collect himself. Faryn's family huddled together where we'd left them, taking great care to not look like they were watching, and Frankie was crying into Finn's chest.

I ran a hand over my face, as all the secrets she'd let out bit by bit came rushing back to me, clicking into place.

It was Lia who'd done this.

Which meant, if what he said was true, that she'd known even as she said it, that she'd done it to herself.

And I'd left her the gun.

What if I hadn't? Would she still be alive?

It broke me apart, all over again, and I couldn't breathe. I'd never known what it was to cry like this, until that night I'd found her bleeding out. And now I didn't know if I'd ever be able to stop.

Spencer produced two tissues and handed me one, then finished his story over my sobs. "It pushed her over the edge, the big to-do my family wanted. It was so stupid, I was so stupid. How could I have thought that wouldn't throw her? She was skittish about marriage in the first place, what with her dad and losing her parents. I'd promised her no kids, but anything that reminded her of them, of the loss, her childhood, her father…"

Through my tears, I managed out that it had been my gun. I'd brought it to her, handed it over, and may as well have killed her myself.

"Lia had been searching for peace for a long time," Spencer muttered. "After she left, I realized she'd stopped taking her meds, months before. Maybe this was her last shot, letting Faryn take over completely. She'd been suicidal so many times..." He got choked up and couldn't finish, but he wasn't talking about Faryn. He was talking about someone else.

I couldn't think of her as someone else, and I refused to. I had known Faryn, and she had been perfect. He could cry for Lia all he wanted, but to me she was just who she was.

Soft waves of hair on a soft face, with beautiful brown eyes and plump, rounded lips. She spoke gently, moved gracefully, and was the piece of the puzzle I'd been missing and searching for my whole life. It didn't matter her name. It mattered I loved her.

And it mattered she was gone.

AUTHOR'S NOTE
Contains Spoilers

This novel was born from my healthy respect for the power our brain can hold over us, and how desperately we can sometimes wish we could climb out from beneath it—not only in the matter of Dissociative Identity Disorder, but even when not facing a diagnosable mental illness.

Apologies that Faryn's story ended in tragedy, but as I neared the climax, I didn't see any other way for her path (being a fictitious suspense novel) to resolve. Trust me, I've spent a lot of time imagining how she and Kai could live happily ever after.

According to the Merck Manual, Dissociative Identity Disorder is associated with a "high incidence of suicide attempts" and these patients attempt suicide more frequently than other psychiatric patients, as they often have other illnesses they're simultaneously battling. A study of 100 DID cases in 1986 reported that of the 71 who'd made suicidal gestures, 53 were internal—one alter against another. Of these 100 cases studied, there was only one death.

That being said, I've witnessed how much brighter a future than Faryn's can be had in the face of mental illness, and hope that falling in love with her throughout this novel—though she held her cards close and was not the most reliable of narrators—might help, rather than hinder, society's sensitivity to mental illness.

ACKNOWLEDGMENTS

I'm going to start at the beginning and try to tackle everyone who left a piece of them with me, pieces necessary to my development as a writer and the creation of this book. First, a thank you to Marian Tomberlin, without whose enthusiasm I may not be writing today. Thank you for cheerleading me on so resolutely when I took those first steps so many years ago.

Thanks in large doses to my husband, who has shared me with my writing for a long time now. Thank you for letting me be me, even when that me is wandering off with a thought in the middle of something or getting all angsty because it's been too long since I sat at my computer. Thank you for all you do every day to make my life more pleasant, which gives me the space to do this thing I want so desperately to do. I know I don't say it enough, but I mean it all the time. Thank you, thank you, thank you, you are the very best.

Thanks to all the writers and editors who've helped me hone my craft over the many years such a thing takes—Kat Abbott, Paul Ullom-Minnich, Angie Stanton, and Mairead Ahmed, to name only a few. Thank you Mary Silva, for long ago telling me that sometimes you have to shit or get off the pot. Though it took me years to listen, your words have been prodding me along since this particular venture began to form in my brain. Thanks also to Gina Ardito for her fine-tuning, and Chris Slabber—because holy cats you guys, *this cover*.

A final sincere thank you to all who've read this book, because stories are meant to be shared, and it would be pretty lonely sitting in a drawer.

"…Mercer's prose is lucid, and her themes of redemption and reinvention are resonant…"

— *Kirkus reviews*

"Gwen's and Betta's storylines will appeal to fans of women's fiction, while Ez's narrative will satisfy those looking for a coming-of-age story. Overall, readers who enjoy family sagas will find After They Go an engaging read."

—*OnlineBookClub.org*

"There's plenty of engaging drama. There are lovers, sibling rivalries, petty jealousies and devastating self-doubts."

— *An IndieReader approved novel*

About The Author

J. Mercer grew up in Wisconsin where she walked home from school with her head in a book, filled notebooks with stories in junior high, then went to college for accounting and psychology only to open a dog daycare. She wishes she were an expert linguist, is pretty much a professional with regards to competitive dance hair (bunhawk, anyone?), and enjoys exploring with her husband—though as much as she loves to travel, she's also an accomplished hermit. Perfect days include cancelled plans, rain, and endless hours to do with what she pleases. Find her on Facebook @jmercerbooks or online at www.jmercerbooks.wordpress.com.